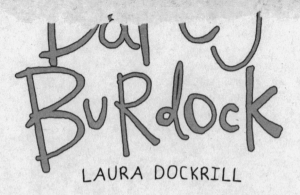

BuRdock

LAURA DOCKRILL

www.**randomhousechildrens**.co.uk

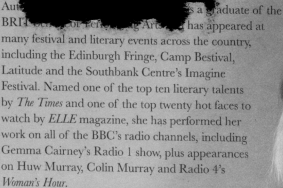

Aut... ...s a graduate of the BRIT School for Performing Arts and has appeared at many festival and literary events across the country, including the Edinburgh Fringe, Camp Bestival, Latitude and the Southbank Centre's Imagine Festival. Named one of the top ten literary talents by *The Times* and one of the top twenty hot faces to watch by *ELLE* magazine, she has performed her work on all of the BBC's radio channels, including Gemma Cairney's Radio 1 show, plus appearances on Huw Murray, Colin Murray and Radio 4's *Woman's Hour*.

Laura has been a roving reporter for the Roald Dahl Funny Prize, and is on the advisory panel at the Ministry of Stories. She lives in south London with her bearded husband.

Darcy Burdock is Laura's first book for children. After having her stage invaded by fifty rampaging kids during a reading of her work for adults at Camp Bestival, she decided she really enjoyed the experience and would very much like it to happen again. Laura would like to make it clear that any resemblance between herself-as-a-child and Darcy is entirely accurate.

'Everyone's falling for Laura Dockrill' —
VOGUE

Darcy Burdock

CORGI

DARCY BURDOCK
A CORGI BOOK 978 0 552 56607 0

First published in Great Britain by Corgi Books,
an imprint of Random House Children's Publishers UK
A Random House Group Company

This edition published 2013

5 7 9 10 8 6

Typeset in 12.5/15pt Baskerville MT by Falcon Oast Graphic Art Ltd

Corgi Books are published by Random House Children's Publishers UK,
61–63 Uxbridge Road, London W5 5SA

www.**randomhousechildrens**.co.uk
www.**randomhouse**.co.uk

Addresses for companies within The Random House Group Limited can be found at:
www.randomhouse.co.uk/offices.htm

THE RANDOM HOUSE GROUP Limited Reg. No. 954009

A CIP catalogue record for this book is available from the British Library.

Printed and bound in Great Britain by
CPI Group (UK) Ltd, Croydon, CR0 4YY

For Daniel,
the greatest story I have ever known

Chapter One

Have you ever noticed you're noticing? Sometimes I notice that I notice so much that I get trapped in noticing my noticing. I like noticing all kinds of things. The way Dad always steals sheets of ham out of the pack in the fridge and thinks nobody sees him do it. The way our next-door neighbour Henrietta

gets so embarrassed
after she's told us
off that she hides
behind the
washing line
and pretend-
innocently hums the
tune to one of those soaps

my mum watches. The way Cyril, the man who lives
across the road, always
looks the woman
in the flower
shop in the eye
for ages and
ages like they
are the only
two people in the
world that count –
even though Cyril has
a *Mrs* Cyril, so *obviously*
don't say I told you.

This is called noticing, I guess.

This book is made for noticers. The curious ones. You know – the ones who peep through spy holes when they're not meant to. The ones who nose into people's front rooms on their walk home from school, the ones who pretend they are doing up their shoelaces when really they are sneakily listening in to a conversation. Of course, this book isn't for *everybody*. Like how mushrooms aren't for me, well, here is who this book is not for:

Boring people

and

Donald Pincher

and

Jamie Haddock

and

Young babies

I am Darcy and I am ten but so nearly eleven. I have long hair that I never brush that everybody

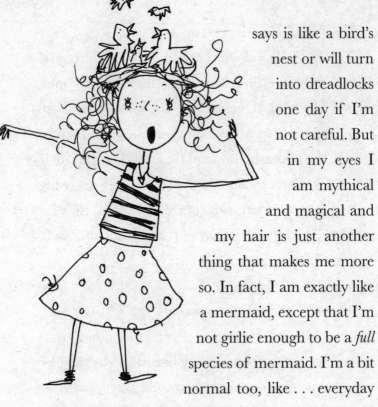

says is like a bird's nest or will turn into dreadlocks one day if I'm not careful. But in my eyes I am mythical and magical and my hair is just another thing that makes me more so. In fact, I am exactly like a mermaid, except that I'm not girlie enough to be a *full* species of mermaid. I'm a bit normal too, like . . . everyday marmalade, so it makes me a mermalade (mermaid + marmalade = mermalade).

Mermalades sit on sofas on the seashore, with unbrushed hair, reading Japanese Manga and eating peanut M&Ms, and when anybody has any danger mermalades will immediately splash into the sea and

4

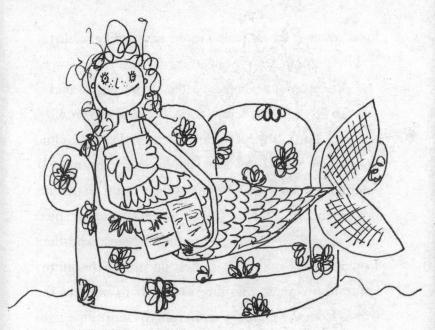

be a hero. We can breathe underwater for hours – no, *years* – without stopping. We blow air into the mouths of anybody who needs it, but obviously not mouth-to-mouth because that makes a kiss, so we put a willing seashell in between our mouths and the drowning person's for hygiene reasons. Of course, being a mermalade has its advantages, and although I love it I have to get on with being a normal person too. Plus mermalades was a much more fun game when

I was younger. These days, I mostly just get laughed at.

I desperately want to be a writer.

I dream about being a writer for whiles on end. I save up my pocket money – well, if I *get* pocket money, which I don't always, either because I've been too naughty or Mum forgets or Dad doesn't want to break a tenner because he's feeling stingy – and I spend it on notebooks . . . That's if I haven't already spent it on chocolate or pic 'n' mix or bangers. And then I open up the first new freshest page and I write my name in my neatest writing. Dad says I write like the waiter from the Chinese restaurant, in short little tight squiggles like the sad trail a spider would leave after it's found itself drowning in a pot of ink and has helplessly clawed its way across the page in persevering agony to get to safety.

This is my first book. One day this book will be published, and that means it will be on people's bookshelves and in libraries, and people in the library can read it. But not snotty drippy babies or annoying geekazoids. It will be read by people like you.

my writing book

I read all the time too. I want to write books like the ones people have on their bookshelves. With spines that say my name. I asked my dad if he thinks I will and he said, 'There's no reason why you shouldn't. You watch the world and make it yours.'

So basically, that's what I'm doing. I'm just watching.

I like painting my fingernails different colours.

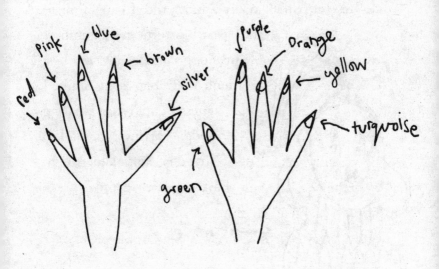

red
pink
blue
brown
silver
purple
orange
yellow
turquoise
green

I like the Discovery Channel; there was a thing on about octopi once. There was this one purple octopus and he looked so sad and lonely and I felt so sorry for him; imagine having all those arms and nobody to cuddle them with? I've got a big sticker of a purple octopus on my writing book that my Uncle Adrian got me from SeaWorld. At the moment octopi are my favourite creatures. I like socks that have a different compartment for each toe. Octopi don't have toes. I hate shopping at the moment because I'm too big for all the kids' clothes and I can't fit into adults' clothes yet, which really annoys me: I can't wait to start wearing turtle-neck jumpers and hoop earrings like my best friend Will's big sister, Annie. I guess I could start wearing hoop earrings, but I'm currently not allowed to have my ears pierced.

← Annie

I once kicked a seagull because it knocked my ice cream off my cone. Dad refers to it as 'not my proudest moment', but WOW, have you ever tried kicking a seagull? They are *hard* to kick. So ultimately I am secretly proud of myself actually. I don't really like birds that much anyway, because they spend all their lives feeling sorry for themselves and squawking. I like bugs much more. I have a spider living in my room at the moment. It has a fly in its web but it's not eating it. It's weird. I can never leave food on *my* plate. If I ever find a bug in our house I always remove it and concentrate so hard not to kill it.

I have punched one person before, and now *that's* something I'm not proud of. And I don't even know why I did it. Well, of course I know why, I just don't know why my hand wasn't listening to my head at the time. It was Jamie Haddock. I still know him and he's still a wretched, wicked person, but I'm not allowed to go near him because I punched him.

Which I am fine about, but he always still comes over and tries to talk to me.

He doesn't seem to care one tiny bit that I punched him. I punched him because he cut a butterfly's wing off with a pair of scissors. I think if you saw that happen with your own eyes then you'd probably punch Jamie Haddock in the face yourself. I didn't get in too much trouble, mainly because my school know that I'm a good girl and have morals. Plus they know Jamie Haddock is a nightmare . . . He has even made a teacher cry before, so maybe I punched him on everybody's behalf?

I like trying on costumes and wigs in fancy-dress shops. I am a master of disguise. I like riding my BMX bike with Will. But I like girl stuff too. Once I even got a braid put in my hair in Spain. But I only got it so I could get that fat heavy bead at the end to flick at my sister Poppy. I love going on holiday to places with water because I am a terrific swimmer and will never mind taking on the role of shark when necessary.

I go to school. But everything seems to be about boring old school these days so I'm staying away from that dry place as much as possible in my writing book. It's a nice fine normal school. We have an excellent plant in a pot in our class called 'Tina' that we all love and take turns to water. We even sometimes get to draw her in art. School is so *normal*. We do all the subjects and I have lots of friends, and no, I don't eat the school dinners —

I bring packed lunches. Once or twice my packed
lunch has included a slice of left-over pizza from the
night before which is SIIIICCCCCCKKK. Jamie
Haddock always hates me even more on those days
as he always has boring Dairylea sandwiches.

And, errrrr, before you ask: no, I don't have a boyfriend. After the way Will's big sister got her heart cracked into a trazillion million billion pieces by that idiot boy Chad (can I just say, who on earth is called *Chad*?), I thought, *Errr . . . naaaaa, darling, romance ain't for me.* I got my heart set on Eminem anyway – nobody else at school fancies him because they say he is old so I think I have a chance.

I shall now tell you a bit about my family.

My mum is adopted. But I hate this word, *adopted*. It makes my mum sound like she was one of those kids left in a picnic basket on somebody's doorstep like an unwanted knuckle of bread. And she wasn't. She isn't a knuckle of bread at all. Not one bit. Whatever your favourite food is, then that's what she is. My favourite food is . . . well, I want to say something really posh like Ferrero Rocher ice cream, but I can't because I've never had that ice cream and so that's lying and you're not allowed to do lying, so really it's probably just fried eggs and chips, and that's because you get to burst the egg and watch the

yellow river running out like an eggy sunshine flood and the chips are the people that need to escape the flood but sometimes their time is up and they've got to surrender to the yolky goodness. Yum. Mum doesn't think about being adopted too much. I know this because she doesn't really nag on about it. Not like Marnie Pincher, who's always moaning. Now she's an example of somebody nag-nag-nagging.

Instead, Mum says she wants to make our lives the best ever, which I feel like she actually *can* do. Not like those people on TV shows that go 'it will change my life' because going on TV does *not* in *no* way make you have the best life ever. Mum says when she had me

an amazing wonderful terrific rare jewel thing

it was like she was searching for shells on the beach one day and she stumbled across the most wonderful beautiful preciousest rare jewel, and that was me. I came by surprise. I'm not stupid – I know that means I was an 'accident', but sometimes the best things in the world are accidents.

I have one sister and one brother and I am the eldest. This means I am the one who has to help out the most but I am a really good mother hen. I've been told this more than once, but I've also been told that I am 'as much use as a chocolate teapot', and I have to say, I preferred *that* compliment.

Hector is the youngest one. He is five. I am really annoyed because I preferred it better when he was a baby. I would wrap him up in 'swaddling clothes' (i.e. a spare duvet cover, a curtain, a tablecloth or, if desperate, a towel) and would leave him (just for one small second) under the dining-room table, and then I would get into character, pretending I was a maid from the Victorian times out on my usual errands. Then I would find the poor orphan (my brother) all by himself; left crying, helpless, rejected. Of course, it was my duty to help him because the character I was playing was once an orphan herself and had made a promise that she would always take care of any baby without a mum. It was always a wonderful theatrical performance, and I would have to hop all over the living-room furniture to get us to safety. Obviously the sofas were drawbridges with mad frenzied crocodiles snapping at our feet and the rug was a huge fire pit. Sometimes Mum would shout, 'Put Hector down!' but I was *that* good at improvisation I wouldn't let it throw me or drop character, I'd just whisper to him, 'I'll never

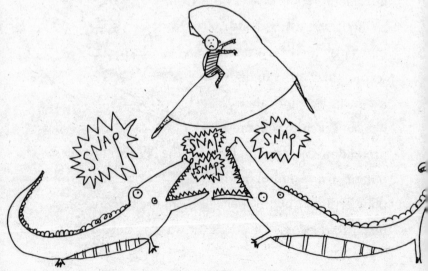

let them take you away from me.' I'd say it dead in character, real breathy and believable, so I was the best actress in the period drama and Mum was the baddie.

When Mum stopped that game because 'it's too dangerous' or 'Hector needs feeding', I would go right into her room and dress up in one of her *smasual* (smart + casual = smasual) dresses and attend the Oscars. I would use one of her posh perfume bottles as a prop and pretend it was a gold statuette. I'd always win one, of course. I'd do my speech in the mirror. I often cried. I liked watching myself cry in the mirror.

Now Hector is five, and he likes zombies, eating snails and anything to do with snakes. He likes Coco Pops in the microwave and jumping off the wardrobe onto the bed.

He also loves (he doesn't) most passionately dressing up as a girl (he doesn't, he hates it), and whenever possible he says, 'Please, Darcy, dress me up as a girl.' Sometimes it's too difficult to say no. I just can't, not to a face like his.

My sister is eight. Her name is Poppy and she wants to be a dancer. She dances all day long. Sometimes I watch her, which is good, but if I'm annoyed and

hear her banging footsteps tapping out the wrong rhythm it's like an elephant hurricane in my mind that drives me bananas. I'm not sure if this will make sense or not, but she is my best and worst person in one body. Sometimes I look at her and think how proud I am that's she's my little sister. Other times I see her skipping on her skipping rope and I just want to trip her up so badly and smash her teeth all out onto the floor – is that bad?

I have got a best mate, but he's a boy. His name is Will. Everybody used to laugh and say he was my 'Prince William', but now they don't because they know if they do I will accidentally-on-purpose spill PVA glue on their heads in art. It's happened before and it can happen again.

And basically, between us, my dad is just good. He is like

the dads you see in the park, forever untying the tangled knotted string on a kite, never giving up, always ready to give it another go.

And that's us.

The best thing about me isn't actually me. It's my lamb. And that is strange, I know, because I live in South London and not on a farm, but she's more like a curly dog. She loves food and strokes and eating Dad's smart shirts (she has expensive tastes) and she's *cool*. Her name is Lamb-Beth. This is because she is a lamb from Lambeth. Lamb-Beth sleeps in my room, curled up like a tiny teddy. She never bleats like those annoying sheep on TV. I don't what they're always moaning about. I don't know any other reason why she doesn't bleat other than she simply must be a super-lamb. Which she *is*. Or maybe she has nothing to complain about?

Dad always makes the most horrible jokes about

her, like, 'What's for dinner tonight, Darcy, roast lamb?' or, one summer, he went too far and picked her up pretending to put her on the BBQ. Lamb-Beth didn't even bleat then, not once. But it was a joke. Maybe she knew it was a joke? Anyway, I hated Dad more than ever that day. I ran to my room and he chased after me, saying, 'It was a joke. I'm sorry, Darcy.' And I slammed the door in his face so hard, and when I slammed it I imagined I saw his fingers being trapped in the hinge. I saw blood hissing everywhere and his big fat paw rammed into the wood. But not really – I knew it was a joke and we did become friends again.

But the worst thing about it all, about every single bit, was that Will was there and he *laughed*. And for some reason, even though my anger had passed and I wasn't angry with Dad any more, I was still furious with Will. I couldn't even look at his stupid face. He said, 'I knew your dad was only messing around.' But still, even though I knew too, I didn't stop hating him and only now – and I mean actually *only* about a day ago – would I even let him be on his own with Lamb-Beth. Not that I thought he would suddenly pop her on the BBQ, but because I wanted to punish him. It wasn't easy because if there's one thing Lamb-Beth loves, it's Will. She can be so naïve.

Chapter Two

We have a new girl at school. Now, I know I *promised* promised not to make this about school, but in every life there are crossovers. And anyway this isn't even about school; this is just to set the scene. She's an American girl, which at first I thought was cool because I saw her as a bit of a gateway to happiness, since *Glee* comes from America and the best horror films come from America and gangsters come from America, and it seems that most delicious food comes from America too. But the more I got to know Clementine, the more she annoyed me, and that's when I remembered about all the yucky stuff that comes from America, like mayonnaise and

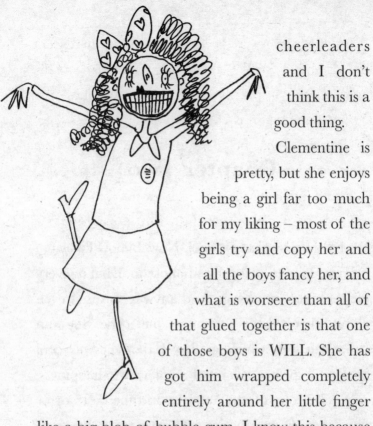

cheerleaders and I don't think this is a good thing.

Clementine is pretty, but she enjoys being a girl far too much for my liking – most of the girls try and copy her and all the boys fancy her, and what is worserer than all of that glued together is that one of those boys is WILL. She has got him wrapped completely entirely around her little finger like a big blob of bubble gum. I know this because whenever Will tells a joke, which is usually one of my jokes recycled and then concealed to be his by a few minor adjustments, she does this ridiculous laugh that sounds like a donkey eating Crunchy Nut Corn Flakes.

But the truth is – and everybody can see this except for love-blind Will – that Clementine is actually laughing *at* Will and not *with* him. BIG difference. Which in my maths is Clementine = a brute.

Clementine has been getting up my nostrils for a while now, irritating me like a sneeze that won't come out, until finally it's all too much for me to handle.

Over lunch, Will says this: 'I'm going to see if Clementine wants to get a McFlurry after school.'

I dig my yellow painted nails in fury into my peanut-butter sandwich (which I normally am not allowed to have, but the cheese had blue dots on it so Mum had no choice) and try to be nice and show interest.

'What flavour are they doing at the moment then?' I avoid eye-contact with him and fiddle with the sticker on my Granny Smith apple.

'Creme Egg.'

'Yuck. I hate Creme Egg,' I bite back, as though an evil black snake has wiggled into my ear and is sitting inside my brain and telling me what to say. And then I slam my sandwich into my lunch box, making the most fuss I ever could, and walk away. I have tears in my eyes because I am cross that Will would like a complete wretched beastly brute monster like Clementine, and even though I am walking away from Will I can see, through pretend magical eyes in the back of my head, that he is confused, sad and disappointed.

Later, on the way home from school, Will catches up with me. He has a handful of strawberry shoe-

laces, which are medium to extra-large amounts of enjoyable, and I say, 'Sorry.'

'What about?' Will asks, lowering a shoelace into his mouth and tipping his head so far back it looks as though it could yank off his neck at any moment.

'Earlier. When I was weird.'

'You're always weird.'

I chew my shoelace. It's gone soggy in all the places where it was sat on my hand because I am sweating a bit.

'Why do you want to have a *McFlurry* with Clementine?' I ask.

''Cos she's pretty and she comes from America.'

'Will, everybody thinks she's pretty and comes from America.'

'Well, that's 'cos she *is* pretty.'

BLUGH. BLUGH. BLUGH. BLUGH. BLUGH.

← Get out my brain.

The black snake crawls back into my ear.

'*I* don't think she is,' I snap. I flinch, which proves I'm lying, I think (which you're not allowed to do, remember), so I change my tune and say what I think he wants to hear. 'I think that could be nice. You should ask her.'

His little red face lights up and I can hear the drum of his heart parading like a float of musicians at a carnival.

Now what you need to know about Will – although possibly, obviously, maybe he is the coolest boy I've ever met – is, he isn't really 'eye sugar'.

Let me tell you how to make a Will:

1. Take a troll.
2. Stretch out the troll's face so it is nearly as wide as a dinner plate, being careful not to confuse the wideness with fat because it isn't. It's all rock-hard bone. Will has a sharp face with extreme features as though an architect carved it from wood.

3. Cover in gingery, fox-like, squirrel colours for hair.
4. Scatter in freckles.
5. Pop in two green mossy conkers as eyeballs.

In the winter he wanders beside me like the palest person on the planet, almost transparent he is so milky. But it suits him, and the contrast is excellent with the red and ginger hair. But in the summer – OUCH! If he meets the sun for even a second he looks like a frazzled sausage.

It is now lunch time on the following day. Will has put gel in his hair.

Clementine is sitting on the other side of the dinner room. She has curled her hair today, which to me looks like a pile of overcooked noodles, but I bet the boys are seeing shades of Beyoncé and Shakira. She has an ever-growing circle of boys around her, which makes sense, as they seem to be the only species that can stand her, hanging on her every word like clothes pegs.

'I'm going to ask her right now.' Will suddenly jumps up, patting his ginger hair into place. 'Do I look OK?'

NO, YOU DON'T! YOU LOOK LIKE A MASSIVE CHUNK OF SUN-SHRIVELLED WATERMELON IN A SANDPIT AT A ONE O'CLOCK CLUB. WITH A TROLL FACE STRETCHED OUT INTO A PLATE BUT NOT IN A FAT WAY.

He doesn't. He actually looks the nicest I've ever seen him.

'You look all right,' I say, and then I fall into my elbow and watch him trudge over.

I don't know what he even says or starts to say, but all I hear is a massive cackle from Clementine. A cackle so loud and horrid and haunting it makes me want to cuddle myself and say, 'Don't worry.' And Will, for no other reason than he must think he is Spider-Man, perseveres and starts laughing too.

But he isn't cackling; his is more of an awkward snort. And it's even more awkward that everybody knows he has attached himself to a joke like an unwanted bit of Velcro on a favourite wool jumper.

This isn't good. The laughter spirals down to a dead end and then Clementine murders the atmosphere entirely.

'Hey, whatever your name is . . . why don't you just go away?'

'Oooooooooooooooooooooooooooooooo . . .' say the other boys in deep chorus. 'That was harsh.'

Will walks over towards me, head in the sleeves of his over-sized jumper. He is as purple as the octopus on the Discovery Channel.

'That *was* harsh,' he gulps. Then slumps.

'Want to get out of here?' I help.

'Yes, please.'

At home, later, I feel bad. Not even just for Will. I feel bad for Clementine. How sad for her that she thought it was cool to be that cruel to somebody, especially somebody who was about to ask you if you wanted to have a McFlurry with them, even if it was a Creme Egg one. Especially somebody as kind as Will.

I decide I need to make light of the situation. I take out my writing book; I keep seeing Will's purple embarrassed face in the front of my memory, staring at me like a letter that needs to be urgently taken to the postbox. *I am going to write a love story,* I think. *A love story with a happy ending.*

THE OCTOPUS STORY

Open your eyes.

Now close them.

Now open them.

Now . . . close them.

(Now open them, silly, or how are you going to see the pictures?)

Imagine this lady. Go on, you have to imagine this lady.

This lady has beautiful long brown hair as soft as a posh towel, as shiny as tinfoil.

This lady has beautiful eyes as blue as your tongue goes after a blueberry ice pop, as shiny as tinfoil.

This lady has beautiful skin, as tanned

as something really tanned or as though she
had been standing next to a toaster for far
too long.

Now this lady was so breathtakingly
beautiful that people had to keep a spare bit of
breath in their necks in case she walked by.

This lady was so beautiful that nature loved her too. Nature curved to her, swayed to her: tree branches would clamber towards her, the river to the bank, the sea to the shore, all in hope of being as close to the lady as they most possibly could.

The grass stretched tall just so that her fingers could skim over them. The birds sang for her, the animals called for her, picked fruit for her, made nests for her. The flowers bloomed for her.

When she was hot, the sun melted and the rain poured free and fast. When she was cold, the sun bubbled and boiled and bubbled and boiled and bathed her in its heat.

She really was, as you can probably gather, quite spectacular.

And, of course, being this beautiful meant that the lady could choose any man she desired. Fat, thin, hairy, square, bald, greasy, gangly, hippo-ish, funny, geeky, triangular, mushy . . . troll-like.

But everybody knows that it is very boring being in love with somebody that thinks you're the best thing ever. Being adored can get dull.

I mean, don't get me wrong, she loved the attention; she gobbled it up like it was her big fat bacon sandwich in the morning. The more everybody stared, the more she strutted. The more she strutted the more they dribbled, and the more they dribbled the more she glowed like an angel.

One of the beautiful lady's favourite things to do, when in need of a confidence boost or simply being a little bored, which was every morning at exactly eight a.m., was to wander down to the sea.

Now, it was a known fact that the lady was terrified of water – especially the huge roaring ocean.

So sometimes she would trot along by the seaside and dip one freshly painted royal blue toenail into the sea and then she would go . . .

'AHHHHHHHHHHHHHHHHHHHH!' (drama-queen scream.)

To which a pack of sea creatures would rush immediately to greet the lady, whether that be dolphins, salmon, crabs or whales, and in unison they would cry:

'Do not be scared, fair lady, of this sea so cold and vast and blue,

You are the most wonderful being in the whole of the world –

It is us that should be fearful of you.'

And in return the lady would gush and applaud their performance and skip, satisfied, happily away.

And today was no different.

After their spectacular performance, all of them yelping out their most favourite parts of the morning's recital, Octopus crept out from his cave.

'Gentlemen of the sea . . . I know that this may come unexpected to most of you, and so I apologize in advance for startling any of you. Tomorrow, when the most wonderful lady in the world comes to sea, I wonder if . . .'

He began to get nervous, his tentacles flapping wildly like a flag in violent turbulent winds. 'I wonder if you may let me arrive for her.'

'Yes, of course,' cried Crab. 'I don't know why you don't come up with us all the time.'

'Yes,' agreed Electric Eel, 'you should join us.'

'No,' hesitated Octopus, braving and holding his nerve. 'I want to arrive . . . *alone*.'

'ALONE?' cried Whale. 'Are you mad?'

'Are you crackers?' called Squid.

'Bananas?' insulted Shark.

'Listen, Octopus,' blew Blowfish, 'you are a good guy. You are funny and smart, and interesting. But . . .'

'You ain't the hottest tad in the pole, eh?' added Hammerhead Shark.

'I know, but I think she might *like* me,' Octopus stated. 'I truly believe that I love her so much that it will become infectious.'

'No,' Seal said, folding his flippers. 'It ain't fair.'

'Let him do it,' clipped Crab. 'It's not as if she's going to *like* him.'

'That's true,' agreed Eel.

Octopus could barely sleep a wink that night; he was so disgustingly excited about the following morning that his whole body was juddering like a jelly.

The other sea creatures laughed at Octopus preparing his jokes, and a sardine let him rehearse his wink in the reflection of his shining body.

The sky went from a light hollow emptiness right through to a deep dark black that was swallowing all the day; the sea became cold and harder and each bubble spot on the surface hurt like the cuts you get on your palms and kneecaps when you fall over on the pavement – *ouch*. Eventually the rising sun split through the jacket of the night, tore through the cloudy sky like pink and orange gas, and the heat glazed the sea, sending spinning golden dust dots through the waves. Octopus let each spot of luck rain down onto his head.

And it wasn't long before morning and he heard the lady's voice bouncing over the subtle splashes of the waves.

And, as nervous as he was, up he went like a rubber parachute, up and up like an elastic air balloon, up and up and up like a chewy umbrella.

And poked his fat head through the roof of the sea.

'Oh,' said the lady, not bothering to conceal her disappointment.

And the Octopus began.

'Do not be scared, fair lady, of this sea so cold and vast and blue,

It is only water, after all . . . so . . . erm . . .'

And at that the lady fell about with laughter, a dirty laugh that made her squeeze tiny tears from her eyes and made her tummy go as tight as the skin on a drum.

'What's so funny?' Octopus asked, trying to join in on the joke.

'YOU! Look at you! Why, you are about the most ugliest thing I've ever seen. What an embarrassment you are! Silly sausage, thinking you could pop your gross bunion head out of the sea and convince somebody of my princess-ish gorgeousness that the sea is not a place full of worry! I shall never walk here again.'

'No! Please come back,' the kind Octopus said,

thinking that his fellow sea-mates would just about pluck his tentacles off one by one if the lady did not come back to visit them. 'I will never come up again to greet you. I swear I will not. Never again will you have to see the pure horrid ugliness that is my face.'

And to that the fantastically beautiful being that is the lady nodded in approval and went to flirt with the fishermen.

For a moment the Octopus kept his head out of the water, feeling the grains of beach salt stick to his eyelids, and he wanted to cry – of course he did, he was in love, after all.

And down he went, like he had a stone in his body. He sank, his tentacles floating, spread out like an empty palm.

He couldn't very well go down to the others and say the lady had laughed in his face, so he lied. He said, 'I won't be going up to see the lady again. She isn't nearly as pretty as I once imagined.'

'Have you lost your marbles?' Eel cried.

'Nope. Not at all,' the Octopus said, before swimming calmly to his cave.

But secretly our Octopus was very smart and knew that even if he was the ugliest thing in the world it was extremely cruel and very unkind to speak to anybody the way that lady had spoken to him, and an unkind person makes an ugly person. He knew that, in his heart of hearts.

The next morning the sea creatures were up with the sunshine, and as soon as they heard the dramatic yelp of the lady they rushed to the surface of the sea to give their recital.

The lady gushed and then said, 'Just out of curiosity, that ugly Octopus – where is he on this beautiful morning?'

'What?' asked Whale, surprised.

'You know, that ugly Octopus – ooh, you must know him for his wretchedness; I felt

46

I was a bit mean to him yesterday. Where is he?'

'He'll be down on the sea bed,' Crab answered, confused (and a bit jealous, actually) as to why such a beautiful woman would be interested to know where such a vile creature as the Octopus was.

' Will you ask him to come tomorrow?' she asked, all flirty, flicking the salty water with her feet.

'He won't come,' Whale replied. 'He doesn't fancy you any more.'

' WHAT?' the lady screamed. 'I don't believe you – go and get him for me.'

The sea creatures swam down to the bed, where they couldn't wait to see the look on Octopus's face when they told him that the most beautiful lady wanted his company (most of them thought it was part of an evil plan to make the Octopus look silly, so they were quite excited, the meanies).

'Nope. Not interested,' Octopus said.

' WHAT?' Crab scuttled.

'I'm not going. If she wants to see me she can jolly well come down here and sing for *me*!'

'You've lost your mind, Octopus!' Whale boomed.

'No, *you* are the ones who have lost your minds! Charging up there the way you do every morning to flatter that silly woman's ego. She may be good-looking, but she is unkind and that is that.'

And then he folded his tentacles across his body, all eight of them, and closed his eyes until they all left.

So on the next morning when the lady heard that Octopus would not be coming to see her, she was quite saddened by this, quite confused, quite oddly destroyed. How could Octopus not be coming to see her? How could he not want to wrap her in his legs and cuddle her until

48

she was a squashy pulp?

The whole day felt so long and never-ending, but she was sure that he'd appear the next day with a weedy bunch of pathetic seaweeds and watery eyes, begging for forgiveness . . .

But he did not.

That day was so long, like a tunnel with no light and no ending, and now she began to lean into the earth like a flower with no petals and no bamboo to hold her up. She kept expecting Octopus to pop his head up and apologize for his shyness, plead for forgiveness for his behaviour and explain how this was all just a muddle of insecurities and he had never loved anybody before and wasn't quite sure how to deal with the emotions . . .

But he did not.

He didn't come the next day or the day after, and the lady, as beautiful as she was, just could not stand this rejection any longer . . .

' WHERE IS THAT OCTOPUS?' she screamed, and stomped her feet and began to cry like a four-year-old in the supermarket who wants a chocolate biscuit. The sea creatures were quite startled. The most beautiful lady had a temper. A temper they weren't sure they liked, actually.

'In his cave,' Crab answered.

'In his cave,' the lady imitated in a particularly mickey-taking, spoiled baby voice.

'He doesn't want to see you,' Shark added.

'Fine,' the beautiful lady, who was swiftly looking less beautiful, snarled. 'Well, in that case, *I* don't want to see *him*, EITHER.'

And she stormed off and tripped over a loose plank of decking and got an awful purple bruise right on her big toe, and then she got up and stormed off again.

For the next three days the lady would try her best to make the Octopus come to see her, as she hated losing. She tried dangling her glossy hair over the water; she tried counting to ten in Japanese and singing in her very best singing voice.

But no sign of Octopus.

She was lost, her aching heart hurt and it made her cry.

Down under the sea the creatures were getting pretty sick and tired of the lady's behaviour. What a nightmare she was with her huffing and puffing and crying.

'Please go and shut her up,' suggested Turtle.

'No, thanks,' Octopus said, shaking his head. 'Not today, not tomorrow, not ever.'

'Please go up and see the lady,' Dolphin tried.

'No, thanks,' Octopus said. 'Not until I've died, been fried and am served up to her.'

When the news came back to the lady she simply couldn't take it any longer. How she missed that Octopus – his silly face, his grimy slimy complexion, his rubbery arms and legs – and when darkness fell onto the sea, like a drape over a parrot's cage, the lady dived into the water that she was so afraid of.

Her breath held tight, her hair spanning, billowing under the dark cool triangles of the water, she swam fast, her lungs filled, beads of glass on each hair on her skin as though she were made of bubble wrap, and the creatures saw her, and pointed her to the cave of the Octopus.

Octopus watched her from the shadows, his eyes big and dull.

'Octopus?' she called.

But he did not come.

And with her last breath, she gargled this:

'I *was* so afraid of this sea so cold and vast and blue,

You are the most wonderful being in the *whole* of the world,

And so it is *I* that have come down for *you*.'

And then she collapsed into the lashing water, and as her body began to sink, Octopus came out and scooped her up into his eight arms and flew his lady to the surface like the fastest rocket ever rocketed.

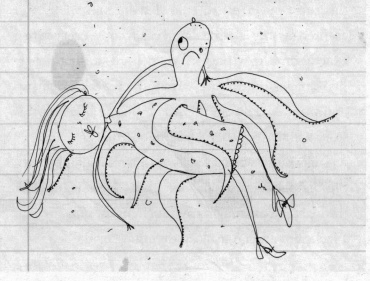

> The lady spluttered and coughed and winced
> and choked and still looked like the most
> wonderful woman in the world, and her eyes
> lit up, and she lifted her arms and brought him
> close, and he brought her close.
>   'And it is I who have come up for you,'
> smiled the Octopus.

I have never had the patience or the time with previous stories to do this before, but all of a sudden I got an instinctive rushing urge to copy this story out. And so I do. I write and write, and as tired as my aching hand is, I copy every word exactly onto new pages. When I am finished I tear these pages out of my writing book, fold them up and print WILL on the front. I have a feeling this story will be very useful to him one day.

I close my writing book and stroke Lamb-Beth. She is falling asleep; her little breaths circling through the air make tiny touchy noises on my ear. I feel calm and go to sleep dreaming of the sea.

Chapter Three

The Pinchers are Mum and Dad's friends. Dad and John Pincher went to school together back in the olden days. Not cavemen and all that, but *old*. Now they are businessmen together, which I know my dad isn't really that good at because he's generous and thoughtful and you're not allowed to be a businessman and be generous and thoughtful at the same time because otherwise sweet and kind ideas pop into your head when you're making crucial money-making decisions. They work with anything to do with wood. Doors, floors, furniture. They do banisters too, and once even a spiral staircase that I got to go and try out for myself. I hated it in the end because the woman kept saying thank you to my dad way too much and stroking his arm, and Mum would not have liked to have seen that one bit and nor did I, to be bitterly honest.

In my brain, the Pincher family wins the award for the world's most annoying family every day, and here's why. Let me tell you about them.

John Pincher is so annoying and huge and goes into the toilet for ages and makes it smell of burning newspapers. Every single button on his shirt is clinging on for dear life against the press of his hot fat tummy. I like chubby people, but I do not like greedy people and this is what John Pincher is. Greedy Gonzalez. He is the sort of

person that says, 'Anybody eating this last canapé?'
(Not that we have canapés, but it sounds posh and I
wanted to set the scene at a posh event so you could
see how bad his manners *really* are.) But he asks it
as the canapé is already at the
stony gates of his teeth, with his
little nails already stabbed into
it. I don't like sitting next to him
because he is the most boiling
person alive.

John's wife is the most
annoying. She is worserer
than a car insurance
TV jingle. Marnie is like a
squawking bird, and remember,
I don't much like birds; her nose is like
a beak, and her teeth are all crunched
together, cluttered and jam-packed like
an overcrowded cabinet of china-ware.
She has a laugh that could make you
want to hurl yourself off a mountain.

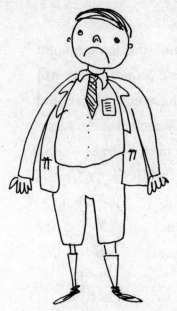

But the most wicked wretched thing about the Pinchers is Donald Pincher.

Who is a . . .

copycat

know-it-all

follower

shadower

. . . with a silly bossy nasal voice and custard breath.

Sometimes the Pinchers come over on Fridays, because if it's been a good week (or a bad week or a medium week or any type of any week) Dad and John Pincher go for a 'swift half' at the pub after work. A swift half is to do with drinking beer. And then, before you know it, Marnie Pincher will be over, all pink lipstick and worrying rattling wrists, dragging with her a fidgety Donald, complaining about Donald's posh school fees and their neighbours' planning permission and boring stuff that I don't care one inch about.

So today is Friday. I am annoyed because I am trying to get on with watching *Spirited Away* with Lamb-Beth. I'm eating Ben & Jerry's Caramel Chew Chew and I don't have that warm excited happy feeling in my belly, like *Ooh it's Friday*, because Mum's 'throwing together a lasagne', and that means the Pinchers are coming round.

Poppy has got the right idea, and has already packed away all her favourite stuff so that when Donald comes over he doesn't start chucking everything around and breaking it.

But I'm on strike.

Ding-dong.

'That'll be them now,' Mum says, licking white sauce from her thumb. She quickly glances at me. 'Darcy, come on, put the ice cream away and at least *pretend* to be happy to see them.'

I like Mum. So I get up and move. I am in the kitchen, I walk over to the freezer and then I hear the squawk.

'Wahhhhhhhhhhhhhhhhhhh!' Followed by the

59

laugh, followed by her clip-cloppy shoes on the hallway floor. 'Smells good in here, doesn't it, Donald?' Marnie chants. Oh, and that's another thing that's irritating about Marnie – everything is: 'Doesn't it, *Donald*?' or, 'Isn't it, *Donald*?' or, 'Don't you, *Donald*?' as though everything needs to be run past *Donald* like he is an emperor sultan king when really he is a *hell* boy.

''S OK,' he grunts. 'What is it?'

'Don't be rude, Donald. Now, off you go and find the gang – no doubt they'll be rioting upstairs.'

She is unbearable. 'Gang' – what on earth? – and 'rioting'? The only person that riots in this house is Donald. I get cross, but am distracted by the thundering sound of Donald's crashing feet stomping upstairs, storming in and out of our bedrooms as though his head was on fire and he was looking for a basin of ice to cool it off in.

I open the freezer to put the ice cream away. The shelves are rammed with fish fingers, oven chips, Mum's collection of home-made chicken stock that nobody ever dares go near, and puff pastry. I put the ice cream on a twinkling, thick slushy layer of crumbling snow, each ice star weaving into the thawed walls like mini diamond snowflakes. I close my ears and eyes and breathe in the cold.

Mum's lasagne is medium to extra-large over-cooked. The corners are all crunchy like my giant atlas book, but it's cheesy and so it's OK. Dad and John are still at the pub, which is worserer than them being at home because it means that Marnie is louder than ever and she is being quite mean as well about John. I spray a heart of tomato sauce on my plate and it squelches.

'Sounds like a fart,' Donald snorts and then copies me, but he's not as artistic so he just does a splodge. He eats with his mouth open. Gross. Poppy pokes her tongue out at him, but before he can tell on her I pretend to choke on my food for one sec and then everybody looks at me, until I have a sip of drink and go, 'I'm fine.'

By now Mum's a bit drunk, so I'm allowed to

be excuse-moi'd from the table. Thank goodness. Hector's hands and hair have got meaty sauce in them anyway, which is gross so I'm happy to be away. I'm going to write upstairs, but I might see if Poppy's up for learning a dance routine off YouTube later.

Lamb-Beth is curled up, sleeping, in my room. I give her a bit of a comb, even though she prefers being knotty like me. It felt like not even a slice of time went by, but I think it did because I noticed it was awfully quiet downstairs, and unless that means Mum's had enough and knocked Marnie out with a frying pan (fingers crossed), something is up.

I go downstairs and that's when I see: Hector softly crying on the sofa, Poppy twiddling her thumbs and trying to be invisible, and annoying Donald hogging the PlayStation like a PlayStation hogger. I go over.

'Donald's not letting me have a turn of the 'puter,' Hector muffles in between sniffles.

'Oi, Donald,' I start. I surprise myself by how ready I am for a fight. 'That car game you're playing? It's Hector's. Can he please have a go – maybe *now*?'

I am right up next to Donald; close enough to see he has tomato sauce on his cheek and poo breath.

'Nope.' He stares at the screen like he's in a zombie trance.

I go red with anger. 'Donald.' I glare at him like my eyes are daggers. 'Give. Hector. His. Controller.'

'Losers weepers,' he says out of the corner of his spitty mouth, which I must say makes me want to shove him. Hard.

'Well, you are such a loser, *you* must be weeping all day then!' I shout.

'What?' he grunts. 'Don't get it.'

'That's 'cos you're so dumb, Donald. *Now share,*' I hiss like a baddie.

'Yeah, share,' Hector cries through little squeaks.

'No. Shut up now – you're distracting me and I'm on level five and I've only got one life.'

'I'm getting Mum,' Poppy suggests, but first she looks her eyes into my eyes to make sure that's a good idea, and *Yes, it is.*

I fold my arms, I squint my eyes and pout. I'm thinking, *Your days are numbered, Donald Pincher, just you wait.*

Mum comes in. 'Oh, Darcy, can't you sort this out? What's the problem? Can't I even have five minutes without you lot hassling me?'

'Mum, Donald is being a PlayStation hogger and he is not letting Hector have a turn of his own game.' I am nearly crying I am so furious. I wouldn't normally be – it's only because of how badly I hate Donald.

'Donald, why don't you let Hector have a go?' Mum tries.

'Because I'm on level five and I only have one life left,' Donald says to Mum in a posh schoolboy voice, like the voices they did at the theatre when we went to watch Shakespeare's *The Merchant of Venice* with the school.

'OK then, Donald, so when you lose your last life, you have to share and pass it on to somebody else, please.' Mum squeezes little Hector's shoulder and gives him a kiss. It is late, I guess; he must be tired and wanting to see Dad.

'Yes, of course, that was my *intention*,' Donald whistles in that stupid voice, and using the word *intention* like a clever Simon Cowell.

'No it wasn't,' I snap.

'Darcy. Watch it,' Mum warns.

'No, *he* should watch it, Mum.'

'Darcy, no back chat,' says Mum, and then she confirms she is giving a warning by saying, 'I'm warning you.'

I am so Angrosaurus rex right now that I don't think; I just open my mouth and scream, 'I hope Donald loses his last life *now*, in *REAL* life.'

And then everybody stares at me.

Shocked.

That is the worstest thing you can do of all things – to wish somebody loses their last life in *real* life. Mum is cross. Mad. Mad. Mad. But so am I.

Marnie comes in. 'What's going on?' she croaks.

'Darcy wished death upon me,' Donald thumps, his red cheeks blaring at me like clown noses.

'No I nev—'

'Yes, you did!' Donald pretend-whimpers.

'Darcy, you need to go to your room and cool off. I'm very disappointed with you and it's clear you've got overexcited,' says Mum.

'*Overexcited? Overexcited?* Is this the way an over-excited person looks?' I say with sarcasm, and drop my jaw and face her blankly.

'Darcy. Enough,' Mum orders.

Poppy looks upsetted.

'But Mum, it wasn't me,' I cry. Because I feel like I'm being blamed for something I didn't do, and now I can't even retrace my steps to work out how it went so wrong. Mum shakes her head at me in disgust.

'I wish Dad was here!' I roar like a lion.

And then what really tips me over the edge of madness is when Marnie pipes up, 'Darcy, don't you think you've upset everybody enough?'

I run upstairs and get out my pen and note-book, and I write as quick as I can about every single word and idea that is in my head. I am ANGRY. I start right away, digging my pen into the paper so hard it leaves traces of every word for pages and more pages underneath . . .

(For maximum effect, please read this out loud in a very fast and angry voice)

You are mad. You are crazy. You are so angry! Even your toenails are furious. Your spine is jagged and in a triangle shape, like a dinosaur, the angriest one of all . . . an ANGROSAUR!

RAHHHHHHHHHHHHHHHHHHHHHHHH!

GRRRR!

The Angrosaurus rex is the craziest, most vicious saur of all saurs. You do not want to meet her. Her hobbies include ripping apart rocks aznd breaking trees.

> *Nobody knows what makes the Angrosaurus rex quite so angry, but it is known, to the best of our scientific knowledge, that when she is angry she is extremely dangerous and her fierce behaviour can be fatal to those that cross her path. Although we can reveal, after proven laboratory testing and sufficient evidence, that a calming aid for the Angrosaur, in an emergency, is Maltesers.*

I breathe hard like I am a runner in the Olympics.

I know I should turn this into something good, like real writers do; you need to use all these annoying things as inspiration.

I write I HATE YOU DONALD PINCHER in massive letters.

I read this back.

I don't think this counts as turning it into 'something good'. So I think long and hard about stupid

Donald. I think long and hard about the PlayStation and the control pad, and then suddenly, in a burst, it comes to me. My story.

Did you know that when you do something too much for too long, fantastic things can happen?

I once knew a man who played the drums every day for furious hours, for so long, so often, that eventually his brain had enough and left in the middle of the night; properly actually climbed out of his head, clambered down his ears and shoulders and escaped. Yep, just like that.

I once knew a woman who drank so many cups of tea every day her teeth fell out one by one and were replaced by square Scrabble tiles with the letter 'T' on them instead of teeth.

But then I heard this. For me, there was no story more fantastic than the story of Donald . . . I mean, *Declan Grabber*.

Declan Grabber and the dreaded car game

It began with an obsession. An obsession so huge it makes me want to write the word 'obsession' like this:

Obsession

But also with a gazillion S's so when you say it aloud you ha<u>v</u>e to really drag it out like this:

Obsssssesssssssssssssssion

Has that made things clearer? I do hope so. Well, that is how truly obsessed Declan was.

But what was he so obsssssessssssed with? you say. And the answer to that was simple.

Cars.

Declan was car-crazy. Every single Saturday his mum took him to the showroom to rub his hands over the sparkling shiny paintwork of the new vehicles.

Every single Sunday, his dad took him to the racetrack to watch the whirlwinding dirt-dust spray mushroom-like humps into the air when a speeding car gushed by.

Declan spent pretty much every school holiday whizzing around the local go-kart track or smashing into the back of some helpless five-year-old on the bumper cars. He was ghastly like that.

Declan was so car-obsessed that he had a car-shaped bed, with a car-print duvet set, a car-shaped clock and a car-shaped rug. Declan had car-patterned pyjamas, a car-shaped toothbrush, he drank from a special cup with a picture of a car on the side and even had a limited edition car-shaped cookie cutter-outer. He was – now I am about to make a small joke

here, so please prepare yourself for immense joy
and laughter – he was . . .

CARazy!

Yes, that's what Declan was.

However, it was odd, don't you think?
To have this obscure, intense fascination with
something he had never actually had the
experience of driving. It was like being obsessed
with macaroni having never once tasted it. So
every day he would pester his mum and dad to
let him sit behind the wheel of their car,
just once; to let him just stretch his foot
out and have a go at pushing down on the
pedal.

And of course, they said, 'No.' They said,
'It's dangerous, Declan.' They said, 'It's
against the law to let a little boy drive.'

And to that Declan would do a sequence
consisting of the most ugliest things you have
ever seen. He would grit his teeth, his fists
would clench, his face would bleach and his

eyes would slit and he would scream, 'I am *NOT* a little boy.'

He had a truly terrible attitude, he really did.

One evening Declan and his doting mum were sitting in front of the TV, finishing off filling up the party bags for Declan's birthday party. Do you like filling up party bags? I quite like it and I quite hate it. I like it because it is a fun job, but I hate it because I get jealous of all the prizes. Declan mostly hated filling the party bags because he did *NOT* like sharing. Every time his mum dropped a toy into the bag for one of his friends (which wasn't many because he was so vile) Declan would try to convince his mum that actually, really, he deserved the toy instead. He was a brute. And usually, to save aggravation, Declan's mum mostly gave in.

'THE *NEW* XTREME MEGA SUPER HARDCORE RACING CAR GAME!' said the TV. It was an advert, a loud, colourful, shouty advert.

Declan's jaw hung loose.

'450 *NEW* LEVELS WITH 1000 DIFFERENT RACETRACK LOCATIONS AND UP TO 200 DIFFERENT MODELS TO CHOOSE FROM!'

Declan nodded slowly, eyes glazing over, watering.

'THIS *NEW* XTREME DRIVER RACING GAME LETS YOU FEEL LIKE THE DRIVER, THE *ONLY* DRIVER! WITH BRAND-NEW EFFECTS THAT INCLUDE A WHEEL HANDSET THAT VIBRATES ON ROCKY SURFACES AND EXTRA SKID CONTROL!'

The screen showed a boy, the same age as Declan, behind the wheel of a car, flying over hills and soaring down clear roads, skidding and flipping.

'OUT NOW! SUBJECT-TO-
AVAILABILITY-COSTS-A-LOT-OF-
MONEY-WILL-PROBABLY-BREAK-REALLY-
SOON-AFTER-YOU-GET-IT-THE-DISC-
SCRATCHES-REALLY-EASILY-ACTUALLY-
AND-IT-CAN-GET-A-BIT-BORING-AFTER-
A-WHILE-BUT-SO-WHAT?-NOT-YOUR-
MONEY-IS-IT?-IT'S-MUMMY'S-AND-
DADDY'S.'

The moment the advert finished Declan looked
over to his mum, first of all pretending to be
shy and coy and sweet; he even tried fiddling
with the button on his car-print pyjama bottoms,
wriggling his toes to look cute, but he knew it
was no good.

'No,' she said. 'You've already handed in
your birthday want list this year.'

'But I NEED it,' Declan whined.

'No, Declan, I'm sorry, you will just have to wait until Christmas.'

And at that, Declan stood up and kicked all the pre-filled party bags over and began stomping on top of them like a wretched ruining hammer. He yelped, 'How come THAT boy gets to drive?'

His mum flapped. 'It wasn't real, darling, it was an advert, for some silly computer game.'

'He was driving, Mum. Do you think I'm stupid?' Declan gave his mum an evil look like a snake might give to a helpless mouse.

Declan's dad rushed in, half on his BlackBerry (a posh phone that for some reason shares its name with a fruit) making busy calls and half talking to his family. 'What's all this kerfuffle?' he asked, looking at his red-faced, sweating son and his cross wife.

'Even though it's my birthday, Mum won't give me what I want,' Declan sniffled.

'Well, what is it you want?' his dad asked

impatiently, putting his hand over the mouthpiece of his phone.

'This new car game I've just seen on TV,' Declan warbled.

'I'm sure we can add it to the list.'

'Patrick!' Declan's mum gasped. 'Patrick, no, we must be firm!'

'Oh, come on, it's his birthday for crying out loud. One more present won't hurt.'

'Thank you, Daddy!' Declan ran over for a hug, smudging his crocodile-teared face into his dad's jumper, leaving just enough space to give his mum a snide sly look.

There is something you must learn about the Grabbers if we are to continue this story. Birthdays in this house are not treated like celebratory events where loved ones gather to applaud progress and growth. In this house, birthdays are treated more like prize-givings, in which case the only receiver is . . . Declan.

And that is that.

DECLAN'S BIRTHDAY I WANT LIST

by Declan Grabber

A remote control car

A new go-kart

A crash helmet

Leather gloves

A pet snake

A car-shaped jigsaw

Top Gear DVD

New trainers (you know the ones, Mum)

A skateboard

A bike

A guitar

A DVD player

A trip to Disney

3-D glasses

An invisible cloak

A horse

A house

Some swans

A milkshake maker
A donut-making machine
An expensive posh watch
A monster on a lead
This new car game *as seen on TV.*

On the morning of his birthday Declan
demanded his presents straight away, and he
ripped them open with fury and impatience until
he found his car game. He didn't even *pretend*
to be interested in the birthday cards, like how
you're meant to do.

Let me tell you, Declan played this car game
for forty-three hours straight, even right through
his very own birthday party, stopping only for
a wee, a drink and a bite of banana split.
His friends came and went, awkwardly piling
up their presents for Declan into a towering
stack behind him. The sun went down and the
moon came up and the moon went down and
up came the sun again, and his hands were

still there, clicking away. What a greedy, selfish, bratty boy.

Every time his mum suggested he stopped, he would shout, 'Shut up' and continue to play regardless, until one time he shouted it too loud and then he began to cough. He passed it off as autumn flu, but that was until the dribble came. And it wasn't a normal dribble from sleeping with your tongue out, or fluffing over your sentences. Nope, afraid not. It was a stringy tar-like thick sludge that erupted out of the back of his throat like black lava. And it messed all down his chin and filled the gaps of his teeth like he had been sucking on the end of a leaky inky pen.

Declan wiped the black dribble from his chin and made his way to bed, moaning that he felt unwell.

That night Declan's sleep was disturbed. He was twisting and wriggling and squirming, but he passed it off as tiredness from the flu — until the belly cramps came. They weren't normal belly cramps either, no, not from overeating or nervousness. No, they were long, aching, grinding churns that came from his gut and sounded like a clanking metally sound.

'What's happening to me?' Declan screamed. 'Mum, Dad, come here, quick!' He spat. Black oil was trickling out of his mouth. He leaped up out of bed and began to run, and he ran down the stairs and out of the front door as quick as he could, dribbling and coughing and spluttering the whole way through his exit. He felt so awfully hot, like he could faint any second, and all he wanted was the cold evening air that the streets of frosty London promised.

Transforming is a very painful experience, but let me try to describe it to you in a way you might understand:

Imagine being pumped up by a football pump through your belly button.

Imagine being run over by a tractor.

Imagine being the skin on a bongo for a second, being constantly slapped and beat upon by a large log.

Imagine being a lump of dough under a rolling pin.

Imagine being a flag on the front of a ship sailing through a turbulent stormy sea.

Imagine being a biscuit baked in the oven for forty-five minutes at 250 degrees.

Imagine being a piece of coal in a fire.

Imagine being a pair of old five-sizes-too-small trousers being worn by the fattest elephant in the world, holding on by a single thread.

Imagine being a nail file.

Imagine being the squeaky toy belonging to a vicious dog.

Imagine being a sausage on a BBQ.

Imagine, for one moment, being a bouncy castle at a summer fete for the naughtiest, jumpiest children in the world.

Imagine being a potato being peeled.

Imagine, if you can, being a banana in a blender.

Imagine being a nail under a hammer.

Imagine being a hairbrush belonging to the girl with the knottiest hair in the universe.

Now triple it. That is how it feels to be transformed.

But that, sadly, is what happened to Declan, the night he transformed into a car.

Cool, you might think. No, *not* cool, not cool one bit. There was a twisting turning sound that happened when his face stretched out, his eyes mangled, squeezing sharply to form two headlights, his ears slicing, moving into mirrors. His body began cranking like clockwork, that same noise you hear when a roller coaster is inching up the big drop; cranking, pumping, honking, zooming, clicking, clacking, until his hands and feet began to expand, blowing up, changing into big rubber tyres. His belly stretched, his skin, now snakelike, appeared shiny and metallic rather than squashy and soft.

This was all over and done with in under twenty-five seconds. His parents were too late to see the change; they had only the shreds of their son's oil-drenched pyjamas, in tatters on the stairs, to hold onto now.

Nobody knows where this mysterious car came from, the one that sits outside the Grabbers' house, empty, sometimes getting a parking fine.

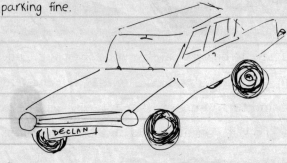

Nobody knows who it belongs to, nor has anybody seen this make of car before. Nobody knows why it has been dumped there, or why it was forgotten.

Nobody knows why that same occasional

spray of water squirts out of the windscreen wipers, all by itself.

But we do, don't we? We know that they are tears — tears from a little boy named Declan, who was CARazy about cars.

I quickly stop writing when I hear footsteps outside my room.

Knock. Knock. Knockiddy. Knock.

IT WAS DAD'S KNOCK.

'Darcy, can I come in?' he says in a softy voice. You have to be very careful with softy voices, because sometimes these lure you into thinking everything is OK and then suddenly you are trapped and before you know it you are being hideously most awfully told off.

'If you want.' I say it meanerer than I meant to.

The door opens and it's Dad, his eyes sleepy and happy. 'What's up, Doc?'

'Nothing.'

'Is that a code word for a certain *Donald*?'

'Maybe.'

'Darcy, you mustn't let him wind you up like that.'

'He was being a horror.'

'Yes, but we can all be a horror.'

'No, but he's the worserest one at being a horror as well.'

'Worse than you?'

'Mucher,' I say and kick my leg, accidentally knocking my writing book onto the floor, and it flops open on the page where I am angry and writing cross things.

Dad looks down to pick the book up, and the big massive letters that say I HATE DONALD PINCHER are screaming in Dad's face and I know he wants to say nothing and ignore it and keep his mouth closed, but he doesn't. He turns the next page and then the next one, his eyes racing at all the words. Then he looks at me and goes 'Oh, Darcy.' But not in a 'poor Darcy' way, in a 'what a real shame that you think and write such awful things, why can't you be good for just simply five seconds of your whole life?' kind of way. And this makes me mad. Madder than what I even was being before.

'Darcy, why are you writing about Donald?' he finally asks.

'It's a story,' I say.

'I don't care what it is. It's not very nice, is it? You wouldn't like it if somebody was writing terrible things about you.'

After realizing he was probably right, I just simply feel even WORSERER, mixed in with embarrassed about the story and my drippy spider handwriting.

So I say, 'Get out now, please!' to him.

And he says, 'Darcy, I don't like your tone.'

So I bark, 'Well, I don't like *you*!' And then I kick my bookcase and two books fall down, heavy boring ones, and this makes everything look more dramatic and worserer than what I actually did in the first place.

'You need to stay up here and calm down. Clearly you are not the grown-up girl I thought you were.'

And then he leaves.

I think about shouting 'SHUT UP' so loud or 'I HATE YOU' but mostly these two ones get you into more trouble than what you were already in, so I whisper 'Shut up' to myself, but that makes me feel no better, so then I try 'I hate you' in a whisper voice too, but that doesn't work either.

So then I know that there is just one thing to do.

Run away. Obviously.

Chapter Four

It is Saturday morning and obviously I already woked up in the worserest mood. I can't believe that even Dad was on Donald's side.

I still feel the same about running away. I packed and everything.

When I go down the stairs I hear Mum singing along to the radio and it makes me happy mixed in with annoyed. Happy because she sings when she's in a good mood, but annoyed because how dare she be in a good mood and just scribble out what happened last night like a cancellation in a diary when my feelings are still so ruined?

I have my rucksack on my back and Lamb-Beth

on her precious going-to-
the-park-lead and I make
heavy crashing stomps
when I go down the stairs.
I know that when people
run away in *real* life they
try and be the quietest
object that ever existed
to not get caught, but

that's when people want to disappear, and obviously
I don't want to do that. I just want Mum and Dad
to feel guilty.

By the time I am done stomping down the stairs
Mum still hasn't noticed me, and so I stomp past

the kitchen and I know she can hear, but she ignores my sound and so I have no choice but to find an excuse to go in and make sure she sees me. I stomp in to get a glass of water, Lamb-Beth trots behind on her lead and I turn the tap on crazy foamy loud like a waterfall.

Mum looks over and says, 'Morning, love. Morning, Lamb-Beth.' She hums and carries on being a mum.

And I think hard hard about something cool and scary to say to show I am grown up and amazing at the same time, but I can't think of anything except: 'Hi.' And that sounded too nice, so then I add on to the end, 'Bye.'

And then I just manage to grab a yoghurt off the side that was obviously meant for Hector, but it's my only chance to sneak.

And Mum says and does nothing.

What on earth? I am leaving and she doesn't even care. This is terrible. Dad's with Hector, watching the football in the living room, and so I quickly run there too. I go in, watch them watching the TV for a second, and Lamb-Beth runs over and starts licking Hector's bare toes. Eugh! Why does she have to be everybody's friend all the time?

I pretend to have an over-dramatic nose-around in the papers on the side.

'What you looking for, Darcy?' Dad says in between laughter with Hector, who is looking like a happy well-fed little joker duck.

Really, I am looking for attention but I panic. 'Passport,' I lie, avoiding his eye contact.

And then what tips me so far over the edge is when Dad not even glances me one more look and just goes, 'Oh, cool.' And then goes back to the football. 'Going anywhere nice?' he teases, but he says it really believably.

AARGH!!!!!! Why doesn't anybody care?

'Right, that's it,' I say to Lamb-Beth. 'It's just you and me.'

Then, after a deep breath, I clip open the catch on the front door and even Lamb-Beth, my bestest thing who loves me more than even sleeping, thinks I'm being silly and her legs stiffen up and I can tell she doesn't want to go. Maybe we should just have a little sit down here on the doorstep to get our bearings.

I see our wretched nosy next-door neighbour Henrietta is watching my every move like a googly-eyed monster spy. She is pretending to wash her car even though it has a bath more times than me. I eat the yoghurt, then bite one of my nails and watch her watching me. If she were a real spy she would know that you have to wear sunglasses for disguise.

I see a cat snaking in and out of the cracks in the pavement, up to something sly. Her eyes are a kiwi green.

And then I see Poppy throwing herself down the hill on her Heelies; she gets faster when she sees me, her big smile charging down the street. She smells like fizzy peach sweets, her favourite, and a bit like mud.

'What are you doing?' she pants, a little out of

breath but with an excited twinkle in her eye.

'Getting my bearings,' I reply, and continue to pretend looking busy getting some bearings. I don't especially know what getting bearings means, but Mum always says it in the car so I know it's to do with maps and roads.

Poppy must have seen Mum do this lots too because she goes, 'Cool.' And then she looks at my stuff and says, 'Then after that are you going to run away?'

'Of course I am.' I stand up straight now; I've had enough of all her prodding and probing. She knows I'm running away because I do this quite a lot.

'Where are you going?' she asks, convinced I'm on the move.

'What?' I get all hot and red. 'Are you a police officer?' I growl and then I feel bad. It isn't Poppy's fault. 'Somewhere far, far, far away,' I say, making sure my voice is softer.

'How far?'

'Basically so far it's not even on a map anyway, not at all.'

'Oh cool, can I come?'

'No, Poppy,' I say, even though of course course course I want Poppy to come, as the adventure would be so dry on my own.

'What's in your bag?' she asks.

'Stuff. Now go back inside. I don't want to screw your life up too.' Ten points for being the best actress in the world (even if it wasn't my best performance, I think we all knew that).

But it didn't matter to Poppy; she broke down into hysterical tears, running inside to Mum and Dad screaming, 'Darcy's running away, and this time I know it's for real! Stop her, stop her, stop her!'

Well, of course, I needed to get going now – couldn't have them find me hanging around on the doorstep. The bearings would have to wait to be got along the way some place else. But then I remember I have no money and that all I have to eat now is absolutely nothing. I begin to feel sick.

I get up and run as hard as I can. Lamb-Beth is so stiff it's difficult to run as fast as I want. I can hear Poppy screaming in the house and I am panicking, worrying so much about everything, oh help oh help.

Then it happens. I have runned so fast I have tripped, and ouch, my knee is bleeding and my hands

have little blistery stingy cuts in them with black stones inside, and now the blood is on my socks and Lamb-Beth is scared and shaking and I have fizzy fuzzy tears filling my eyes and my head is hot and I think I've broken every bone in my body and that I am going to die and my mum and dad don't care not even one bit. And then Henrietta runs out of her front garden and she loops me up into her arms like a small baby.

Ouch, my kneebows, my kneebows. Thank you, Henrietta,

I am thinking. And she says, 'It's OK, dear, don't worry, darling, it's OK.' Like she knew exactly what I was thinking.

And I breathe out loud and say, 'I don't think I will ever smile again.'

And Henrietta laughs and draws me to her warm chest.

Chapter Five

I have been thinking about squashy things for quite a while now. Most of the best things in the world are squashy. Beanbags, fluffy white bread, bed, cake. Big chubby bums.

We are taking some flowers round to Henrietta to say thank you for helping during my mini-escape, which isn't even exactly any of my fault, but still, Mum thinks it is. This is what is in Mum's brain:

Wine
Gregg Wallace off Masterchef
Everything is the kids' fault

Poppy got out of coming because she had stupid dancing class. Maybe I should take up a dance class? Does sumo wrestling count as dancing?

I like the flower shop because if there is one thing I know it is that nature is absolutely beautifully wonderful. Colours are breath-taking. Gold as sparkly as treasure, purples like my octopus and reds like cherry drops, deep inky blues and grassy greens, yellows like glow sticks, pink as pinkie as a piglet. Each petal is different, delicate and amazing. The smell is so fragrant, like nature's perfume. The flower shop . . . I mean the *FLORIST'S* (Mum has just told me off) is extra-good because it has a bell when you go in that tinkers, and then by magic the flower shop lady appears as though she's been waiting like a magician's assistant behind her counter the whole time to pounce 'surprise' on us as the grand reveal. Just in a horrid apron instead of an excellent sequin suit which is always a let-down.

The flower-shop lady has got the best thighs and bum. When she cuts the paper to wrap around flowers her whole bum shakes like jelly but better, but that's only because she's more mahoosive. Cyril, our across-the-road neighbour, has started buying flowers nearly every day now, which is just getting silly because his own garden is looking a shambolic mess. He goes the colour of lavender when he sees the flower shop lady, and his fingers move over petals, touching them so smoothly like he is carefully stirring a spoon into a cup of coffee in a saucy advert. He is tall. Which is a good start. I think the flower-shop lady would suit a tall man. And he doesn't mind one bit about the flower-shop lady's fat, which is excellent news because people are always hating other people because they are chubby. But I think chubby is a brilliant compliment and I'm going to start using it more, so if I call you chubby, remember, it means I'm being *nice*.

'You look so chubby today.'

'Ah, thank you so much, etc.'

See?

Well, I know that the flower-shop lady has got what the school nurse says is a 'complex' because I have seen her in a jogging suit twice already this week, so she's obviously not wanting to be that fat any more. Which is a shame, but Mum says, 'There's nothing wrong with wanting to get fit.'

Cyril comes into the shop just as we are leaving. We don't know the flower-shop lady that much apart from 'How are you? I'm fine' conversations, so we can get out pretty quick, but I have just enough time to watch Cyril start to nervously stutter. He has a square of toilet paper stuck to the bottom of his shoe. Oh, Cyril.

On the walk home I am so sad for Mrs Cyril. I keep picturing her in my head as being the kindest woman in the universe. Baking hot chicken pies for Cyril, warming his slippers on the radiator, sewing missing buttons onto his shirt. Sitting by her mirror making herself pretty for somebody who won't even care.

Knock knock onto Henrietta's door. I don't want

her to be in because I am embarrassed that she helped me yesterday; that she saw me trying to pretend to run away and that I bet I got blood on her nice couch.

We knock again.

Nothing.

'She must not be in.' I look up at Mum, all hopeful.

'Course she's in. She's always in, she must be round the back.'

'In the back!' Henrietta sings from the other side of the house, but it sounds as though she is standing right next to us, her voice is *that* loud. Henrietta used to be an opera singer. Which is why she has a massive voice and a massive mouth and a massive set of boobs.

Mum smiles and rattles us round the house and down the garden path. We lean in past the hedges and holly bush, still shaking wet from the splattering hose.

Henrietta is standing in white tennis shorts and a white bra, frumpy white socks and green flip-flops. She is wrinkly. She has a very deep tan. She is wearing a stopwatch round her neck. She is also wearing a visor. The radio is playing old opera music like she always plays but I have never heard this one. She is smacking a golf club into her cabbage-sized palms.

Gasping, she cackles and spins round to face us. Tiny sweat beads escape her forehead.

'Henrietta,' Mum begins, 'these are for you. From us – well, Darcy. To say, well, you know.'

'Thank you,' Henrietta helps, and wipes the sweaty bristles on her top lip. A bit of her ruby red lipstick smudges a little. 'They are just beautiful! But you didn't need to do that!' She smiles at me and strokes my cheeks and throws the club to the ground. 'Come in for a gin.'

Bleurgh. I hate gin. I never had it, but I know I hate it because it stinks like bleach, and bleach means when Mum says we're going to 'turn this house upside down', and that means me tidying my room.

Mum starts to say something, but then just gets awkward and doesn't, and we follow Henrietta inside. We got Henrietta a beautiful bunch of lots of green things that look like a giant excellent salad.

Henrietta is like a stone sculpture of a Greek god, massive and strong and marbly and victorious. She takes a large vase and is muttering about how gorgeous the flowers are, and she fills the vase deep with cold frothy water while also reaching for the gin. I start to notice she prepares most things in this way; grabs two glasses with one hand whilst getting a lemon in the other, slices the lemon and trims the stalks of the greens, snaps open the lid of the tonic water and clinks the ice in, all simultaneously until the results end in two tall fizzing cocktails and a display of flowers.

Wow.

'And what about you, little Miss Darcy? What would you like to drink? I think I've got a little bit of chocolate milk, will that do?'

I really like this Henrietta. Yes, she's always telling us off, but she is funny and unique and strong and has chocolate milk.

And she saved me.

'How are your kneebows?' she giggles at me.

'OK.' I smile, and she winks back instead of words.

Henrietta is not one tiny bit like Marnie Pincher. She isn't giggly or annoying. She is passionate and smart and deep and interesting. I like her house. It's the same shape us ours but nicer. It's tidy and has a fluffy carpet. She has cabinets with ornaments and photographs in posh shiny frames and everything smells of polish. She has a picture on her mantelpiece. It's one of her and a man, but the man is young and Henrietta looks young herself in it too actually. She is in a wedding dress, and in fact, at first I thought it was an ugly dress, but the more I get to finding out that Henrietta is wonderful, the more spectacular I think her dress is. Henrietta sees me looking at the picture, but she doesn't say anything to me. Where is that man in the picture now?

After we finish our drinks we go back to our house and I ask Mum about Henrietta and why she lives on her own without any kids or any men. Mum says that sometimes people are happy like that. But I don't get it. To be a lonely person seems like the saddest story that I've ever heard.

Dad is making pea soup. The pan looks like witches' brew. Poppy is hula-hooping in front of the TV and Hector is cutting and sticking from an IKEA catalogue. Lamb-Beth is sitting with him and she has a cut-out of an ironing board on her ear.

'Soup is ready!' Dad shouts.

'Just a minute,' I call back, and run upstairs as quick as I can, thinking how wrong I mish-mashed Henrietta.

The Lonely People

What happens to the lonely people?
The ones that never get found.
Do they end up winding into the forest
    trees?
Or get their legs rooted into the ground?
Do they spend all their hours hiring videos from
    video shops
Until the stock runs out?
Or maybe they go to the edge of the world
To build a boat
And hope it will float.

What happens to the lonely people

Under their trays of meals for one?

Do they die cuddling a microwave

Whispering, 'You were my only love.'

Do they learn the words to all the songs?

Memorize their favourite books?

Or perhaps they know the best hiding places,

The dark spots, the crannies and crooks?

What happens to the lonely people?

Do their words fall onto deaf ears?

Who laughs when they fall?

Who listens to their fears?

Do they even speak at all?

Who lets them cry on their sleeve?

Who does them favours?

Who knows what they need?

What happens to the lonely people?

Who reads to them before bed?

Who checks their temperature when they're sick?

Who puts a flannel on their head?

Who asks them how their day has been?

Who waits for them at the station?

Who says, 'You have the nicest eyes I've ever
  seen'?

Who stares at them in fascination?

What happens to the lonely people

At parties and celebrations?

Do they even get an invite at all?

Or does their one get lost in the solar system?

Who do they get to grumble with in the evening
  snow?

Who makes them tea?

Who runs out when the milk is running low?

Who has a present for them under the
  Christmas tree?

What happens to the lonely people

When the moon falls down?

When your door is shut and the stars are out,

When you say goodnight

And say, 'I'll see you in the morning',

Remember, somewhere there's a lonely person
  saying goodnight to a nobody.

I drink three glasses of water before bed, not because I was so thirsty, but to replace all the tears that I must have cried over the last couple of days. My tear ducts feel all dried-up like raisins.

Chapter Six

Being a big sister means there are lots of duties you are in charge of. For example, I am the one who gets to sit in the front seat in the car if we are only with one parent, Mum or Dad. I am the one who has to make the toast if Mum and Dad are having a lie in. I am the one who is in charge when it comes to games, but also I am the one who has to make sure Poppy and Hector brush their teeth properly. I am medium to extra-large good at this job because I like having big strong white teeth like a sharp white fence or a crocodile.

This is how it goes:

1. Hold your brushes out.
2. I spread on the toothpaste. Poppy and I use the spicy grown-up one now like Mum and Dad, but Hector has a pink strawberry jelly one as ours is way too spicy for him.
3. Wash a bit under the tap but DO NOT drop off your toothpaste.
4. Brush whilst I count for exactly up to sixty, without stopping not even once.
5. Spit and rinse and, if you can be bothered, do it again.

Now, today, Poppy has cried to Mum that she wants a turn of being the toothbrush person because she is sick of me being in charge. 'Oh, fine,' I said, in a voice I knew would sound not fine, but I knew Poppy's career move to be toothbrush person wouldn't last long.

So we are in the bathroom in our pyjamas. Waiting because it is taking an absolute eternity for stupid Poppy to dish out the toothpaste, and it is going a bit

everywhere but she won't let me help her. And then she decides she doesn't want a spicy one today, she wants the strawberry jelly one like Hector, and then I am a bit mad really. It all makes sense: she obviously wanted to be the toothbrush person so she could slyly have that delicious toothpaste and make me have the minty grandma one all on my own. Hector is crying because he says to Poppy that the strawberry jelly one is his and not hers. But Poppy ignores us and starts counting. How even dare she brush her teeth with that glorious pudding paste and I get this spicy wretched one, and so this is what happens.

At the bit when we are supposed to spit into the sink, I do not spit into the sink, I spit my toothpaste onto the back of Poppy's head. And she doesn't even notice.

I am feeling a little bit quite bad about this, but I don't say anything. Then Mum notices the tooth-paste in Poppy's hair and she wipes it out. Luckily she says, 'Maybe let's wait a bit until you're ready to be in charge of brushing teeth.' And that is that. I will sleep well tonight, I think.

Sorry, Poppy, but sometimes that's the way the cookie makes crumbs . . . or something like that.

Chapter Seven

Stupid Jamie Haddock has mostly been reminding me of hell. I can't wait for the school holidays to happen because being in the same universe as him is driving me dotty. And yes, I know I said no school mentions in this writing book, but I am crazy mad with him.

Jamie Haddock is a complete dandruffy bogey-picking waste of space. I hate his guts, and even though you are not meant to say 'hate', I actually hate him. Mum says, 'If a boy is mean to you it means he fancies you.' That only makes things worse. Jamie Haddock and me have been at school to-gether for TOO long. He reminds me of spit, anchovies, fish, mushrooms, olives, rice pudding and rats. I hate him. More than ever.

Picture the scene.

Will and I are eating our pudding in the dining hall. As I said, *usually*, of course, I bring a packed lunch. But Dad had to drive to work extra early and Mum is looking after Poppy because she sharpened her finger with a pencil sharpener and a roll of skin came out the end and there was blood everywhere. Ha. It was quite brilliant. So Mum said that today I had to have yucky school dinner, because she didn't have the 'patience' or 'energy' to make my lunch.

The choice was:

Cheese flan. *Yuck*.
Chicken stew. *Yuck*.
Or fish fingers.

So I had fish fingers obviously, and actually it was

OK. But it came with shrivelled-up dried peas that looked exactly like bogeys.

We are now eating the only bearable bit about school dinner. Chocolate cake. And we are arguing. We are arguing about how you can make the cake last longer because, it must be said, it *is* delicious. So Will thinks if you take huge massive spoonfuls it will take you longer to chew, making the cake last longer. I think this is stupid. I believe that little tiny spoonfuls, big enough for only a bird, are best to sustain the eating experience. I think, actually, Will agrees with me, but he is being stubborn.

We are watching Caroline and Fabien on the other table. Caroline is special, because she comes from China and has only lived in boring England for a few months, and she is gentle and precious and can make origami out of anything, even toilet paper, and I really am focusing on being her friend right now when I am not writing or being angry with somebody stupid. Fabien is just a boy in our class who is fine and nice, but he is in love with

Caroline these days and I think they are having a date. Then, out of nowhere, over comes bounding crashing bulldozer Jamie Haddock with that look in his eye that means he is out to ruin something.

He goes right over to Caroline and Fabien and goes, 'Awwwwwwwwwwwright, lovebirds?'

And then Caroline flashes embarrassed red and sips her water, and Fabien is a bit shy too and he wears glasses that go steamy when he is nervous.

So Haddock starts some more. 'Have you kissed her yet, Fabien?' Caroline, I think, will cry in about one sec, and Fabien is breathing heavy and hard.

I am mad now and so is Will. He shouts, 'Oh, bore off, Haddock, and go and find some worms to play with.'

And then Jamie looks up and he is mad now too. Jamie Haddock, differently to Donald, is scary because he is unpredictable. As annoying as Donald is, he is simply spoiled and that makes him wretched: he doesn't know how to share.

But Haddock is not spoiled. He has nothing. He

has shoes with holes in them, his clothes are stained with food and Coca-Cola splashes and his nails are dirty. He is always in trouble for stealing the felt-tips in school or trying to take home other boys' coats. His mum is never there to collect him after school.

Sometimes I feel sorry for Jamie Haddock. But not right now, clearly.

'Will, leave him,' I say as Jamie starts to lunge towards where we are seated. Jamie does this thing when he is cross. He huffs and snorts through his nose like a raging bull, he bulks his shoulders up all big and square like a giant wardrobe and charges. He does that now.

Will is so smart and cool he finishes off his last bite of cake and then he sits back in his chair, calmly chewing. This makes Jamie crosserer.

'Do you know what, Will? You are a *real* idiot, do you know that? I've never liked you.' Jamie is talking so much into Will's face, and Will just blinks and shrugs. This makes Jamie louder and madder. 'Say something then, ginger nut.'

'Oi,' I say. 'Stop it, Jamie.'

'Oh, so your girlfriend has to protect you now, does she? Come on, Will, man up.'

'Jamie, I am *not* his girlfriend. Just go away.' I look at Will's empty crumb-littered bowl and then down at my cake. I can see the dents from the tiny spoon marks, like a cliff face, all rocky and brown and scrumptious. Jamie clocks me looking at my bowl.

'How come you left all your pudding, Darcy? Don't you want it?'

He's trying to scare me, but secretly I am so

haps because I've obviously won the cake-lasting competition – a small victory, but one all the same.

'Give it to me,' Jamie says, and before I can even protest, his hand cranes down like one of those metal claws in the teddy machine at the arcade. Snatching it away, he tips his head back and drops the cake into his gargling gob, mushing his lips over the wedge.

Will jumps up and starts shouting at him, then they begin angrily pushing and shoving each other,

backwards and forwards, forwards and backwards, and the sounds muffle out and finally disperse into nothing in my head. All blurring and blending and making only nonsense. I can see Jamie forcing a dramatic swallow as my cake slides down his skinny neck, and as I spot the freckles of cake remains scattering the emptiness of my bowl, I can't stop thinking about how thirsty Jamie is going to be after that because everybody knows forcing cake down your throat in a rush is dry work and certainly needs a drink.

On the walk home past the world, my hatred for Jamie turns into feeling sad about Jamie. Why does he behave like such a hog? I am holding Mum's hand and am thinking about how lucky I am that I have one of these to hold onto and pick me up from school.

'I didn't see Will in the playground today,' Mum starts.

'No. He's in trouble,' I say. My eyes follow Poppy

on her scooter; she's got quite nice balance.

'He is? Why?' Mum asks.

'He had a fight.'

'Oh dear, that doesn't sound like Will. What happened?'

'I don't want to talk about it right now this second if that's OK.'

'Of course that's OK.' Mum is good like that.

Chapter Eight

Lamb-Beth can tell that I am a bit thoughtfully sad.

And I know Mum spoke to Will's mum on the phone, but she still says nothing to me. She senses I'm sad, same as Lamb-Beth. But things look up after I eat some pasta.

'This Jamie Haddock . . .' Mum starts as she scoops up Lamb-Beth onto her lap. 'You must remember that he has lots of things going on his mind that make him very upset.' Her voice is gentle; sometimes I think she should be the voice that reads the ingredients of shampoo on the adverts. 'He doesn't see the world the same as we see it.'

'Yes, well, why?' I ask. I sip my apple juice. 'It's like

he wants to ruin every single thing that's beautiful.'

'Yes.' Mum nodded and smiled. 'I know it seems like that. He isn't lucky like you and Poppy and Hector.'

'Why, though?' I know what she is saying, but I can't be bothered to hear the lecture about how lucky we kids are again and again, over and over, and that we get loads of presents and have a roof over our heads and, most importantly, have 'love'.

Mum looks at me for a while and then she says, 'Because it's hard to love others if you have not been loved yourself.' And at first this is a bit confusing and then I understand and I feel so sad – so sad I think I could die right now.

'Are you saying nobody loves Jamie Haddock?'

'No, I'm saying there is a reason behind everything; you see how Jamie's behaviour is peculiar? I am saying, be patient and sensitive to that.'

I'm not sure I like hearing about how much Mum's trying to make me be friends with Jamie Haddock when he's clearly a hooligan.

'Are you on his side?' I ask.

'No, no, and there's no sides. I just want you to see the bigger picture. And mostly . . .' She's struggling and thinking it's like back to when I was seven and everything was a jumble and she had to explain things a thousand times. She gives it another go. 'You know, sometimes the most wonderful things get overlooked – or, not overlooked . . . what do I mean? *Misread*.'

I am listening to Mum and I am taking it in. Maybe she is right?

'I think I need to go upstairs for a quick sec,' I say, but really I need to write.

The Dandelion's Wish

A story about giving everybody a chance (even Jamie Haddock)

If a dandelion could be heard it would probably say something like, 'I am not horrid.' It's funny how the word EAR is in HEAR but not everybody listens.

All I know is sometimes, maybe, perhaps there is something spectacular extraordinary about weeds and sometimes, maybe, perhaps it's OK to trust them.

Some weeds go around for ever believing that they are the worstest thing on the whole planet, being nothing but a nuisance to absolutely everybody by ruining gardens and practically *inviting* snails to come and munch up all the good stuff, but actually people sometimes don't know enough about weeds to actually even judge. And so maybe if they knew a little more they wouldn't be taking it all out on the weeds in the first place.

Here is a crash course on weeds:

There are the ones you don't touch because they have got something, for some reason, against you and they make you wet yourself and they look like this:

There are the ones that don't mind you so much so you can eat them. They are healthy and you can put them in salad and even in tea and they look like this:

And then there are these really special ones that love you so much you can wish on them; you know the ones that have the heads of snowflake fluffy starry cotton-wool pompoms? They look like this:

Well, these are the ones I want you to imagine in your head right now.

Now these are the Dandelion Wishing Rules:
1. Choose the dandelion with the fullest head of hair; don't pick one that has already got some fluff missing because the wish might not work as well.

2. You must pick from the very, very bottom of the dandelion stalk, so nearly at the root. You will know if you get the right bit because you will hear a noise like this — 'OOOUFT.'

3. Twirl it in your fingers whilst you think of your magical wish; remember to be careful what you wish for because wishing is a dangerous art.

4. Concentrate hard on your wish, say it to yourself and move your lips a bit, but not too much otherwise people might think you are crazy.

5. Blow. Hard.

Whilst spinning the dandelion, watching all the mini umbrella bits float away and scatter into the sky.

N.B. Apologies if you already knew how to do that.

And here we have a huge beautiful field, stretching like a beach of green, studded with hundreds of snowy-headed dandelions. And on top, trampling through, are a family, all stomping and bumping and trudging through the fresh tickly grass.

First the mum of the family looks around and picks the best-looking, healthiest dandelion she can find. She plucks it from the root, waits to hear the 'OOOUFT' sound and then she closes her eyes and makes her wish.

'I hope I get to meet Johnny Depp,' she whispers.

Next, the dad of the family finds himself a nice big dandelion, he plucks it from the root, has a little smile, waits to hear the 'OOOUFT' sound and then he too closes his eyes and makes his wish.

'I hope I don't get stung by a bumblebee whilst I'm here, because there are lots flying around and I am scared and might scream and then my wife and children will laugh at me,' he whispers.

And then all three children do the same. They each find the healthiest-looking dandelion, they each pluck it from the root, wait for the

'OOOUFT . . .'

'OOOUFT . . .'

And, seconds later,

'OOOUFT.'

And the children close their eyes so tight, thinking about all the wishes they need granting.

The eldest goes first, finding a quiet spot slightly away from her family. Although it is a bright day, it is quite cold and very windy, so her hair is blowing wildly and she has to make her wish fast before the wind stole it from her.

'Hmmmm.' She closed her eyes and began to spin the leg of the dandelion. 'I wish I could go on *The X-Factor* and win it.'

And then she blew the head off the dandelion, watching the mini umbrellas tumble into the thick sky, over the grass, the bushes and eventually over the roofs of the little houses that sat next to the field.

Next up was the second eldest. He was really eager and desperate to make his wish and the wind was firing his dandelion all over, and bits and pieces of the dandelion were sticking to his lips and made him look as though he was wearing a chapstick that had previously belonged to a bunny rabbit, so he quickly made his wish:

'I want to eat only McDonald's for every meal for ever and drive a monster truck by myself with nobody ever helping me.'

Pleased with his wish, he began to breathe in and he was trying to blow, but it was turning more into spit. He kept trying, until eventually he managed to release a big huff. It was accidental but it worked, and off his wish went.

Last was the youngest. She was worrying about this wishing business. Of course she could think of things she could wish for: to be an artist, to have a constant supply of strawberry jam, to not have to sit next to that crying boy in school . . . but they just seemed so silly. As she looked out and down on the other dandelions, all waiting for their chance to have a go at being chosen, she suddenly thought, *Well, who on earth do the dandelions wish to? If everybody makes their wishes to them, when do they have a chance to wish anything for themselves?*

And after this she quickly realized that maybe she didn't really need to wish to be an artist at all – maybe she should try hard at school and become one the right way? And although all that jam would be nice, she would probably soon get sick of it. And that crying boy at school sometimes shared his Skittles with her, so he wasn't *that* bad. And what if – what if suddenly all these dandelions had been overlooked? And what was their purpose? To sit here all day long waiting to be wished on? What sort of life was that? And when she spiralled her dandelion in between her finger and thumb, sheltering its woolly head from the wind, she made up her mind.

'I wish that the dandelion's wish would come true.'

And then she blew as hard as she could and her wish was granted, up and over the grass, fluttering past a running dog and dancing over the trees.

'That one must have been a big wish,' her dad said as he watched her dandelion fall apart like a popping bubble and leave, creeping into the sky, travelling much further than the others in the spiralling wind.

'Not really,' she shrugged and, slowly padding in her squashy boots, joined the rest of her family and their walk back home.

I'm not sure if any of those wishes came true. I am not a psychic. I couldn't say if Mum went and had a cappuccino with Johnny Depp, if Dad spent that evening nursing his sore thumb from a vicious queen bee sting or not, if the eldest is sitting sipping champagne with Louis Walsh while watching her brother drive around in his monster truck.

But I hope the dandelion's wish, which was simply to be heard, came true . . .

Chapter Nine

At school the next day I have a home-made brownie in my lunch box and am thinking about what Mum said yesterday. Something makes me leave it in Jamie's tray with a note saying, *From Darcy*. It's not that I think he's starving or anything, but doing nice things for other people grows only gold in your belly.

Besides, it's only chocolate.

I have been thinking about my sister. Poppy can reach her big toe to her eye. With even a straight leg. I can't. Poppy can do all the rap bits to all the songs I like even betterer than me some days. Poppy has got a freckle that is half on her lip; I have freckles all over my nose like toast crumbs. Poppy has got neat perfect hair; I have messy screwball-mish-mangle-tangle hair. Poppy can bend all bendy because she is a dancer; I am like a rigid, short, unbendy crayon. Poppy has a cute giggle; I have a big mammoth drum belly laugh. Poppy looks like an angel girl mermalade friend when she cries; I look like a moose-beast. Poppy says to me, 'Darcy, did you ever realize you are amazing?' She is quite odd.

I have seen a mermaid tail in Poppy's wardrobe that *wasn't* there before and *is* there now and I know it's just a tail and I am all growed up now and said I didn't even care about silly mermalade things any more, but this has actually upsetted me to a new higherer degree. She knows mermaids are MY thing. I don't get why she has a tail and I do not. More than that, she has hidden it which makes me even more angry.

I look at Lamb-Beth. She is cleaning her armpits with her tongue. I wish I could clean my armpits with my tongue.

I am lucky to have a lamb and I guess Poppy's mouse Sylvester did die. But he was a rubbish pet anyway because he didn't really like any of us and he ran away every time he saw our hands going into his cage to pet him. One day he didn't run away, but he bit Poppy and blood came so we stopped trying to pet him, but he even hated us if we were giving him food and water so we stopped doing that too. But without telling Mum. And when she found out she was horrified and said I was lucky to keep Lamb-Beth after the terrible way I treated animals. She said she was going to write a letter to report us to the RSPCA and we were scared and we all hated ourselves and I still to this day don't know if she actually told on us or not so sometimes it's like I'm living my whole life in fear of the RSPCA throwing me and my brother and sister in prison. So now I always take care of every animal.

Breathe.

SO I decide to be a growed-up big sister not caring about silly petty issues like 'Poppy has a mermaid tail and I don't' (even though it makes me want to set her bedroom on fire), but at breakfast my birthday comes up in conversation and we are talky walky talking about what to do for it. And what do I want? And then I get all winded-up because I think, why did Poppy get a *no-reason* present? It was her birthday months ago and she is so spoiled.

So I just say it: 'Well, why don't you ask *Poppy* how *she* would like to spend my birthday, seeing as she's the main one?'

'Erm, pardon? Sorry there, Darcy? What was that?' This is Dad's new tone with me, which means he is treating me like a person and not a daughter.

'Well, I didn't get a *no-reason* present,' I grumble, but already I regretted opening my mouth and hoped I could sew it right back up.

'A no-reason present? What are you on about?' Mum starts the rampage.

'A present for no reason. Poppy got one,' I say, chewing on a toast crust.

'No, she didn't get a no-reason present, and quite frankly I don't think you are in any position at all to start complaining about presents seeing as it's your birthday next week.'

Well, that shut me up.

Poppy crunches down on her Marmite on toast like she is an innocent cute Tinkerbell and I am a troll under the Billy Goat Gruff bridge. We all say nothing.

At school, Will is being all 'HAHAHAHAHA, be my best friend, everybody, and let's leave Darcy out,' and is cracking jokes with all the boys and has even got football boots on. Idiot. And even precious Caroline from the magical land of China is doing trampoline at lunch time and I'm not allowed to join in because I haven't ever turned up before and the beastly gym teacher says I can't 'pick and choose'. Bounce. Bounce. Bounce. Yawn.

But I still decide to spend approximately seven minutes glaring into the gym, wishing I could join in, watching everybody going up and down, and regret not being more open in my advances towards making Caroline my best friend instead of Will.

At home later on, Mum, Dad and Poppy are all drinking hot chocolates and whispering under their breaths and planning a secret gang plan to evacuate me from the planet. I know this because they go 'Shhhhh, shhhhh' when I come into the room.

The next morning I am looking for a hair bobble to tie up my hair, and in Poppy's room I see a bottle of purple hair dye that I never seed before. I am so victoriously outraged. I bet they are gently turning Poppy into a mermaid to make me feel lefted out.

Then, after school, I catch up with Will. I say,

'Hi, Will, feels like I haven't seen you for ages, are you OK?'

And he says, all nervous, 'Yeah, good.' And walks up his speed to get away quicker.

Oh no. What did I do wrong?

I say, 'Will, do you wanna go and get some crisps?' And he says nothing and walks *faster*.

He is always hanging around other people now and not me, and it's not that I am jealous because I love Will or anything, I am just sad, but also when I think about it more, maybe I am just jealous but still not because I love him. I just . . . well . . . Will's mine, isn't he?

At home that night we are having scrumptious risotto, which makes me feel a *bit* better. But still nobody has said anything more about my birthday and it feels way too late to even bring it up, and it's now in two days and I still feel wretched sore and hurting about Will.

Now my birthday is in one day and nobody has even

asked me a single thing about anything. Everybody is just getting on with their own lives and it goes on like this for what seems like an *ever*. I only see Will once at school, and he is talking to a girl called Jemima in the corridor who normally I never even think about, but now she sticks out like a sore thumb and seems like the coolest person ever and I think about her all day and all the walk home until in my brain, suddenly, she goes from being a normal yellow pencil to a multi-coloured paintbrush that I can't escape from my head.

I am starting to feel so outrageously jealous and so incredibly forgotten.

I feel like everybody is trying to throw me out like a pair of old shoes.

Alfie, the Cat and the Hairby Wairby Itchy Witchy Warmy Cosy Over Nosy Never Frozy Navy Greeny Always Reliable Frumpy Wumpy Smelly Jumper

This is Alfie.

'All right, Alf?'

And this is
Alfie's Hairby Wairby Itchy
Witchy Warmy Cosy Over
Nosy Never Frozy Navy
Greeny Always Reliable Frumpy
Wumpy Smelly Jumper.

Here is a gallery of them together:

Here they are watching a film.

Painting.

Baking.

Bathing.

As you can see for yourself with your very own eyes, Alfie and his Hairby Wairby Itchy Witchy Warmy Cosy Over Nosy Never Frozy Navy Greeny Always Reliable Frumpy Wumpy Smelly Jumper went absolutely everywhere together. In fact, there was never a day when they were not together.

But of course, because there never was a day
when Alfie and his Hairby Wairby Itchy Witchy
Warmy Cosy Over Nosy Never Frozy Navy
Greeny Always Reliable Frumpy Wumpy Smelly
Jumper were never not together, the Hairby Wairby
Itchy Witchy Warmy Cosy Over Nosy Never
Frozy Navy Greeny Always Reliable Frumpy
Wumpy Smelly Jumper sometimes got damaged.
From either:

the wool getting caught on the gate

or

a loose stitch in the collar

or

a moth nibbling on the sleeve.
And so the Hairby Wairby Itchy Witchy
Warmy Cosy Over Nosy Never Frozy Navy
Greeny Always Reliable Frumpy Wumpy Smelly
Jumper often needed fixing.

Not only this, but because Alfie and the
Hairby Wairby Itchy Witchy Warmy Cosy Over
Nosy Never Frozy Navy Greeny Always Reliable

Frumpy Wumpy Smelly Jumper were always
together every single day, the Hairby Wairby
Itchy Witchy Warmy Cosy Over Nosy Never
Frozy Navy Greeny Always Reliable Frumpy
Wumpy Smelly Jumper was very dirty and very
smelly.

But because the Hairby Wairby Itchy Witchy
Warmy Cosy Over Nosy Never Frozy Navy
Greeny Always Reliable Frumpy Wumpy Smelly
Jumper was very old, Alfie never wanted to put
the Hairby Wairby Itchy Witchy Warmy Cosy
Over Nosy Never Frozy Navy Greeny Always
Reliable Frumpy Wumpy Smelly Jumper in the
washing machine in case it destroyed the jumper
altogether or, worse . . . shrank it! So it simply
never got washed.

Now what you must know is that
deodorants, bars of soap, air fresheners and
extra brushing of teeth are all excellent masks
for wretched smells, but when something like
the Hairby Wairby Itchy Witchy Warmy Cosy

Over Nosy Never Frozy Navy Greeny Always
Reliable Frumpy Wumpy Smelly Jumper is
around, and has never seen the inside of a
washing machine, a smell like that becomes very
difficult to hide.

Especially when everybody else smells of
normal things.

Alfie's mum smelled of:

coffee and Vivienne Westwood perfume

and

Alfie's best friend smelled of:

chocolate and washing powder

and

Alfie's grandma smelled of:

White Musk and cigarettes

and

Alfie's cat smelled of . . .

well . . . actually, a bit of wee – bad
example, but he is a cat.

But Alfie's Hairby Wairby Itchy Witchy
Warmy Cosy Over Nosy Never Frozy Navy

Greeny Always Reliable Frumpy Wumpy Smelly
Jumper smelled of none of these. It smelled of:

old rainwater

and

wet dog

and

manky soup

and

football mud

and

cheesy feet

and

farts.

And because Alfie and his Hairby Wairby
Itchy Witchy Warmy Cosy Over Nosy Never
Frozy Navy Greeny Always Reliable Frumpy
Wumpy Smelly Jumper were never apart, Alfie
started to smell of these things too.

And after a while it made his life quite
horrid.

His grandma would say, 'Can't you

throw that awful thing away?'

And Alfie would say, 'No.'

And Alfie's mum would say, 'How do you put up with that terrible smell?'

And Alfie would just shrug and say, 'Just get used to it.'

But everybody everywhere soon began to avoid walking past Alfie in the street, and his mum would have to wear a clothes peg on her nose in the evenings when they watched game shows together.

And his grandma stopped baking him cookies.

And his best friend stopped coming round to see him.

This was no way to live. Not at all.

This is Alfie's cat.

There is something you should know about cats.

They are excellent at being selfish.

So when Alfie's cat could no longer take the ghastly stench of the Hairby Wairby Itchy Witchy Warmy Cosy Over Nosy Never Frozy Navy Greeny Always Reliable Frumpy Wumpy Smelly Jumper any more, he didn't hop out of the cat flap and get a breath of fresh air. Instead, he decided to hatch a nasty plan. A plan that would get rid of the Hairby Wairby Itchy Witchy Warmy Cosy Over Nosy Never Frozy Navy Greeny Always Reliable Frumpy Wumpy Smelly Jumper once and for all.

Plan A

Alfie is eating his cereal at breakfast, crunch, crunch, crunch, when the cat hops up onto the table and, with his slinky tail, carelessly (deliberately) knocks the neck of the milk bottle and tips milk all over Alfie and his Hairby

157

Wairby Itchy Witchy Warmy Cosy Over Nosy Never Frozy Navy Greeny Always Reliable Frumpy Wumpy Smelly Jumper.

Alfie leaps up, covered in splashy sploshy milk. 'Oh yuck. Thanks a lot, Kitty,' he grizzles, and tidies the mess. He clears the milk off the table and mops the floor, but does he wash the Hairby Wairby Itchy Witchy Warmy Cosy Over Nosy Never Frozy Navy Greeny Always Reliable Frumpy Wumpy Smelly Jumper?

Nope.

So now he also smells of sour milk.

The cat and his plot have failed. He will need to think of another way to get that jumper ruined.

Plan B

So it is later that day when Alfie is watching TV, chewing a massive blob of pineapple bubble gum, chew, chew, chew, that the cat seizes the opportunity to scuttle over and try, for a second time, to get rid of the vile jumper. At the exact moment when Alfie blows a massive balloon-shaped bubble of gum, the cat lifts his paw and claws a giant gash into it, causing it to burst and splatter all over his Hairby Wairby Itchy Witchy Warmy Cosy Over Nosy Never Frozy Navy Greeny Always Reliable Frumpy Wumpy Smelly (milk stained) Jumper, leaving a sticky yellow mess.

'What is wrong with you today, cat? Look what you've done now!' Alfie is cross and goes to the kitchen, but not to clean his Hairby Wairby Itchy Witchy Warmy Cosy Over Nosy Never Frozy Navy Greeny Always Reliable Frumpy Wumpy Smelly (milk-stained, pineapple-bubble-gum-covered) Jumper, oh no.

Just to get a new piece of bubble gum.

The cat is devastated, but just when it seems like that Hairby Wairby Itchy Witchy Warmy Cosy Over Nosy Never Frozy Navy Greeny Always Reliable Frumpy Wumpy Smelly

(milk-stained, pineapple-bubble-gum-covered)
Jumper is *never* going to get washed, the cat
has a final smart, sneaky and selfish idea.

Plan C

The cat turns the heating up. High. He closes
all the windows and all the doors. The
temperature rises, thick and fast, making the air
hot, stuffy, sticky and unbearable. So hot and
stuffy and sticky and unbearable that the cat
wishes he could unzip his fur like a hoodie and
take it off and slink into a sink of ice-cold
water, and just before he goes stir-crazy Alfie
mutters, 'Wow, it's hot in here.' And fans
himself with his hand.

The cat sniggers. Maybe this plan will work?

But then Alfie relaxes again and even has
a little nap, wakes up, gets himself a glass of
juice and sits back down.

It seems that the Hairby Wairby Itchy
Witchy Warmy Cosy Over Nosy Never Frozy

Navy Greeny Always Reliable Frumpy Wumpy
Smelly Jumper isn't going anywhere, least of all
in the washing machine. *Oh, what a shame.*
The cat will just have to move out.

But then suddenly Alfie's cheeks go a
strawberry red, his eyes puffy and sweaty, and
in one quick peel he huffs and rolls his jumper
off and throws it to the floor as though he
couldn't *wait* to get it off.

The cat looks so happy mixed in with
surprised. His eyes peel back like two de-shelled
boiled eggs and he has to act fast, darting
quick as he can over to the Hairby Wairby
Itchy Witchy Warmy Cosy Over Nosy Never
Frozy Navy Greeny Always Reliable Frumpy
Wumpy Smelly Jumper and, using his teeth, he
drags the Hairby Wairby Itchy Witchy Warmy
Cosy Over Nosy Never Frozy Navy Greeny
Always Reliable Frumpy Wumpy Smelly
Jumper right into the kitchen and throws
the crawling stinking thing into the washing

161

machine and shuts the door with a horrendous BANG.

Do you think cats know how to use washing machines? (Yes, I know this cat just turned the heating up, but a washing machine is a much more complicated instrument.) So let's say, for argument's sake, that *sort of*. The cat *sort of* knew how to use the washing machine.

But at least it switched on and seemed to be whizzing round like it does when humans use it.

Round and round and round it spun, the washing machine and the Hairby Wairby Itchy Witchy Warmy Cosy Over Nosy Never Frozy Navy Greeny Always Reliable Frumpy Wumpy Smelly Jumper. The cat watched the whole time, the jumper and its grubby colours turning, the cat not even blinking once.

Hurry up. Hurry up, thought the cat.

Until, finally, the word READY appeared on the little screen on the washing machine, but at the same time a key twisted in the front door: Alfie's mum was home.

'Gosh, it's hot in here,' she huffed, turning the heating off, but when she saw Alfie without his Hairby Wairby Itchy Witchy Warmy Cosy Over Nosy Never Frozy Navy Greeny Always Reliable Frumpy Wumpy Smelly Jumper on, well, she nearly died and went to heaven, but she didn't want to make a fuss or draw attention to it. She squealed, running to the kitchen, where she saw the Hairby Wairby Itchy Witchy Warmy Cosy Over Nosy Never Frozy Navy Greeny Always Reliable Frumpy Wumpy Smelly Jumper in the drum of the washing machine. *Clever Grandma*, she thought – she didn't know what she'd said or done, or how she had cracked it, but she had, and gosh, she was pleased.

She quickly made herself a cup of coffee and sat in peace thinking of all the nice places they could go now Alfie wouldn't smell.

And when Grandma came home, she too thought the same thing. *Oh, isn't it warm in here?*

Yes, she did think that but she also noticed that the Hairby Wairby Itchy Witchy Warmy Cosy Over Nosy Never Frozy Navy Greeny Always Reliable Frumpy Wumpy Smelly Jumper wasn't on Alfie, it was in the washing machine, at long last. That clever daughter of hers. She also didn't know what was said or done, but it was done all right and she was thrilled.

They both went into the kitchen, winking and nudging each other, believing that the other had put the Hairby Wairby Itchy Witchy Warmy Cosy Over Nosy Never Frozy Navy Greeny Always Reliable Frumpy Wumpy Smelly Jumper into the machine. Clever clog.

But when they pulled open the door of the machine, out came the most wretched foul-smelling flood of disgusting soapy water. It was a brownish yellow colour, dotted with crumbs and hairs and bits of biscuit. It looked like baby sick and smelled of dog poo and rotten eggs.

Blurgh.

'Where's the jumper?' Grandma said, holding her nose, using a spatula to fish through the stinky water.

'I can't see it either,' Alfie's mum said, with a hand over her mouth.

The cat anxiously watched them sifting through the groggy water, fingers crossed the jumper wasn't in tatters. Yes, he wanted that Hairby Wairby Itchy Witchy Warmy Cosy Over Nosy Never Frozy Navy Greeny Always Reliable Frumpy Wumpy Smelly Jumper to smell nice, but he didn't want to ruin it for good so that Alfie could never see it again.

Oh, what had he done? How selfish could he be?

'Oh no, wait,' said Grandma. 'I think we have it here.' Then out she foraged the Hairby Wairby Itchy Witchy Warmy Cosy Over Nosy Never Frozy Navy Greeny Always Reliable Frumpy Wumpy Smelly Jumper, and it wasn't smelly, and it wasn't itchy or frumpy wumpy, but it was . . .

Tiny.

'It's shrunk!' yelped Alfie's mum.

'It's teensy,' sang Alfie's grandma.

' What shall we do? He will be mortified if he never sees that jumper again.' Alfie's mum began to gather tears in her eyes.

Grandma had to think quickly. 'He may not be able to *wear* it again, but I'm sure he will still be able to *see* it.' She gave a sly grin to Alfie's mum, and an even slyer one to the cat.

Here is Alfie.

'All right, Alf?'

And here is his cat and his very tiny Hairby Wairby Itchy Witchy Warmy Cosy Over Nosy Never Frozy Navy Greeny Always Reliable Frumpy Wumpy Smelly Jumper.

Chapter Ten

I need a new writing book. Mine is all tatty. I am reading Nigella Lawson's cookbook before bed, because I've realized that thinking about food before bed always gives me the best sleep. It's a heavy book and eventually I need to slide it off the bed with a big wallop.

Lamb-Beth is already snoring. I am always so jealous of how she can fall asleep in no time.

When I open my eyes I do not feel eleven, I still feel ten. I run my hands over my face and it still feels exactly the same. Not wrinkly or anything.

It's my birthday, which means I'll certainly

be eating dippy egg and chocolate birthday cake.

It's raining outside. The rain is pattering against the window but in my head I see sunshine.

'Mooooooorning, me,' I sing and stretch. 'Happy birthday, me.' Lamb-Beth doesn't know it's my birthday so I don't get mad one bit at her for not wishing me a happy day.

I jump out of bed; the heating has been on so it's not too cold. Sleepily I open up my door and wait for Poppy to come and shout 'Happy birthday!' in my face but she doesn't.

Weird.

I make my way downstairs. 'Mum, Dad, it's my birthday!' I call, Lamb-Beth drowsily wobbling behind me. 'Mum, Dad, where are you?'

Very weird.

I go into the kitchen. Maybe they are there, waiting to cuddle me until my eyes explode, and shower me with thousands of presents and feed me smoothies until I officially turn into a fruit basket.

But nobody is there.

'Hello?' I call. I am a bit scared now. We love birthdays in our life. Where is everybody? Oh goodness, is this what happens when you are eleven? Does everybody forget you are still a birthday girl and get on with normal life? Are they going to march me right off to the bank and make me start paying rent? Oh no, will I need to get a credit card and start watching the news? Oh, hell. I hate being eleven, I want to go back in time to ten RIGHT NOW.

I cradle up Lamb-Beth and decide to go into the living room. I will sit there in front of the TV for as many hours as possible, watching a bazillion cartoons and laughing at every bit like Hector does to prove to them that I'm not at all ready to be growed up and that I need more time.

'SURPRISE, MERMALADE!'

Mum, Dad, Poppy, Hector, Will and Henrietta – all the faces I know and love and more, with balloons

of every colour and cakes and a banner saying:
HAPPY BIRTHDAY, MERMALADE.

And they all hug me tight and say 'Good morning'
and 'Happy birthday', which are my two favourite
sayings (as well as 'Merry Christmas') and things feel
so excellent I can't breathe and we listen to back-
in-the day Madonna songs and Beyoncé, and dance
and eat and cuddle and sing.

Mum has made the room all like underwater,
with blue and white balloons, and she has painted a
sunset and propped it up on the TV so it looks like
the sun going down over the sea. It's the best.

Poppy is dressed as a mermaid and has a tail,
but funnily enough not the same one I spied in her
room, and she has purple hair dye in. She looks like
Katy Perry mixed in with Ariel. Wonderful amazing
terrific.

Will says, 'Do you know how difficult it's been

171

not telling you about today? I've had to avoid you all week!'

Oh, relief. I say, 'I thought you didn't want to be my friend any more.'

He looks sad for one second and says, 'Idiot.' And we laugh and he gives me my present. A new writing book. That really is delicious.

Then Poppy brings out a present for me. I tear it open, noticing the wonderful multi-coloured wrapping paper: it's a mermaid tail – the same one I spied in her room, and I am beaming glorious.

It was a present for me all along. I feel a bit guilty. But not for too long obviously, as it is my birthday.

I'd always wanted a surprise party, like what you see on TV shows like *Friends*. It's always amazing to be shown that people love you. Even when you know you already know, it never hurts to be reminded.

Chapter Eleven

Now that I am eleven, I have learned that sometimes people, when they don't know full beginnings, middles and endings to stories, they will make them up. I am not saying this is called 'lying', but it certainly is not telling the truth. So when Jamie Haddock decided it would be – I am not sure: clever? funny? appropriate? – to tell basically the whole of everybody that I put a chocolate brownie into his tray at school because I was in LOVE with him . . . people did a lot of this *making up* malarkey.

All I was trying to do was be kind.

This is what happened.

We are in class talking with Mrs Grey about our

creative writing work, and we are talking about love and everything and how symbolism in love is really important, bladdy-bladdy-blah, and then Haddock pipes up and goes, 'Yeah, well, Darcy left a symbol of her love for me in my tray last week. A chocolate brownie!'

And everybody goes, 'Oooooooooooooooooo', and I turn into a shallow melty muddy puddle, and because it was a secret, even Will goes all red and looks at me like 'NO WAY?!' It's horrible, and I can't take it because then I feel guilty because Will HATES Jamie after their massive fight in the dining hall over eating my chocolate cake. Will stood up for me, and what did I do to stick up for Will? Put a chocolate brownie in Jamie's tray!

I am so embarrassed and regretful that I shout out, 'You wish, Haddock.'

And the worserest thing you can do to somebody who loves winding people up is wind them up themselves, because it's like a roll of Sellotape being undone a thousand and fifty times in different directions and all you end up with is one giant ball of sticky scruffy mess, and this is Jamie Haddock right now.

'Don't lie, Darcy.' He stands up now and he fumbles in his pocket and brings out the little note saying *From Darcy*, and everybody gasps in astonishment.

I go violet and shout, 'Jamie, I did NOT write that!'

Mrs Grey is going, 'Now, now, come on, quieten down, come on, come on.'

Everybody is laughing, because they don't know which one of us to believe, and the laughter is making both of us crosserer and crosserer, and Jamie is getting that thing he does when he turns into that mad angry bull and huffing hot puffs in and out, in and out through his nostrils and squaring his shoulders up.

He shouts, 'DON'T LIE, DARCY!'

And Mrs Grey is running about all flappy like a chicken being chased by a fox and going, 'OK, let's settle down now, folks.'

And Will is looking all surprised and my heart is thumping so hard it's like everyone can hear it. *Shush up, heart! Shush up, heart!*

So I stand up too and I shout, 'Everybody knows *you* are a liar, Jamie Haddock. I would *never* even *dream* of giving you a chocolate brownie.'

And then Jamie Haddock out of madness rips down our music week display that was on the wall, and lots of our classmates get mad because that was their work too, and this makes Jamie more embarrassed and mad so he pushes over all the pen pots and then he goes over to our class plant, Tina, and he lifts his leg high and goes to kick her over and I shout, 'NO!' And then I pick up a rubber (I'm not sure who it belonged to)

off the table and throw it at Jamie Haddock's head and it splats him right on the forehead and rebounds off onto the carpet.

Will smiles, and so do a lot of other people in my class, but Mrs Grey is '*appalled to say the least*'. And sends us straight away to see the Head.

Jamie and I are sitting outside the Head's office, mainly hating each other's guts. Arms folding, legs swinging. We have to go in one at a time to tell the Head what happened and then we go in together and say it all again. My mum is called up from the school phone and the Head really makes me sound like the worst criminal in the world, and then Mum wants to speak to me and she uses all these big words that make me sound like I am one of those people on the news that commits mass murders – words like *devastated* and *mortified* and it's the absolute worst.

All I can think about is how poor Tina nearly got kicked and broken by Jamie Haddock.

But I am so sorry and sad when Mum comes to get me. She is polite and quiet to me in front of the

Head, until the very moment we get in the car. She hisses, 'Put your seatbelt on,' and I do, and then she is shaking her head and squeezing the wheel so tight.

'Mum. I didn't do—'

But she doesn't let me finish one bit. She goes, 'What did I tell you about Jamie Haddock, Darcy? Didn't we just have this conversation only the other day? What do I need to do? Do I need to record myself and give it to you on a bloody disc so you can hear me over and over again?'

I am crying and so mad, I muffle, 'Yes, well, what was I supposed to do when he told everybody in the world that I gave him that brownie as a symbol of my love?'

Mum says whilst she is spinning the wheel, furious, 'Laugh it off? Be mature about it? I don't know, but how about *not* throwing a rubber at his head?'

I know it was wrong a bit, but I had to save Tina. Besides, what an excellent aim I have. If throwing rubbers at people's heads was a sport, I could be up there with the greats.

Chapter Twelve

MY WRITING BOOK IS MISSING.

Missing. Missing. Missing. Missing. Missing.

I have looked everywhere. I feel like dying. That has all my stories inside it. I feel so stupid and empty.

Mum, who is being much nicer now (she changes her tune more than the radio by the way), says, 'Don't worry, love, we will get you another one.' But it's not the same.

I will never ever be able to remember all those stories.

I go to bed holding Lamb-Beth and feeling so sad; sad like I am in an opera, wailing my heart out in Italian.

I need something to take my mind off this tragedy.

'I think Cyril from across the road is in trouble with his wife – I saw them arguing outside yesterday,' Mum says as she mixes up Lamb-Beth's breakfast of porridge oats and sliced apple and carrot.

Well, well, well, I think to myself like a detective.

'DARCY!' Poppy shouts from upstairs. 'Darcy, get here quick!' I run up the stairs; Lamb-Beth slow gallops behind me and hops up onto Poppy's lap. She is at the desk on the computer.

'Darcy, look, it's your writing book, it's going round on the school website. Look, there's pictures of Jamie Haddock holding it.'

'Pops, budge over and let me see.'

And that is when all horrid hell breaks loose. There are pictures of Jamie Haddock holding up *my* writing book. *MY* writing book. And under it hundreds and millions of people have commented things like:

'DARCY 4 JAMIE'

and

'Burdock and Haddock babies to be had soon'

and

'LOVE IS IN THE AIR!'

SICK! BLURGH BLURGH BLURGH!

My face falls, like a painting in the rain and all the colours washed off.

I panic; I don't know what to do. No no no no no no no no no.

'Why's he got your book, Darcy?' Poppy asks.

'I don't know. He must have stolen it,' I say, still in disbelief as I scroll through each picture of him with my book of words, his face in a nasty grimace. *What is he up to?*

'But how? How did he take it?' Poppy asks. She is more upset than I am.

'I'm not sure.' And then I remember. We took turns to go and see the Head to give our side of the story, didn't we? First Jamie, and then me. He went through my bag, didn't he? He took my book!

'And why is everybody writing all this *LOVE IS IN THE AIR* business? This horrid ugly boy isn't your boyfriend, is he?'

'Poppy! Of course not. People have made this rubbish up.'

'Oh, phew,' she huffs.

'MUM! MUM! MUM!' I call out.

'She's nipped out with Hector,' Dad calls back. 'What's up?'

I can't be bothered to explain to Dad, not in detail, and plus I was embarrassed; I didn't want Dad seeing all this *lovey-dovey* rubbish. He knew my book was missing, but he would be so angry that he would throw a real anger fit like a WWE wrestler if he saw that pimplehead Haddock had taken my book. And why did he steal my book anyway? What good was it to him to have a bunch of my brilliant fantastic amazing stories? Was it to bribe me or something? I'd have to wait until Mum got home. But what if by then it was all too late?

Poppy suggests that to take my mind off things until Mum got back, Lamb-Beth and I might like to watch her rehearse for her dance competition at school. We do.

The very moment we hear Mum's key in the door we both run; pulling her shopping bags out of her hands, practically ripping her coat off her back and dragging her to the computer.

'What's all this about, girls? Come on, can't it wait?'

'No, Mum, it's Jamie Haddock, Mum . . .'

'No, Darcy, I don't want to hear that boy's name in this house. Not tonight, do you hear?'

'But Mum, please.' I push her into the chair in front of the computer. Her hands are all cold from the outdoors wind and I squeeze them. 'Mum, he has *stolen* my writing book.'

'You are joking!' She shakes her head and knits her brows close together like they are two magnets. 'How do you know?'

'Poppy found it on the school website,' I say, feeling so much better now that she is taking this seriously.

'It's true, Mum, I saw it. He's showing off and everything,' Poppy says, typing his name into the search bar on the website.

'How dare he? When did he manage to do that?' Mum squints her pretty eyes at the screen.

'He probably had a chance when I was explaining

my side of the story to the Head,' I say. I feel a bit like we are an all-female police detective squad, hammering down on a crafty villain. Ha. The tension builds.

'Well, if this nasty little boy has stolen from you, my Darcy, there is going to be trouble,' Mum spits.

'I can't find the pictures.' Poppy panics. 'They were here before and now they are gone.'

'What do you mean?' I take the mouse and start flicking through the photographs. 'I don't under-stand. How can they just disappear like that? What about the comments everybody wrote?'

'Nope, not here either.' Poppy bites her lower lip.

'Where have they gone?' Mum asks. 'Look, girls, are you sure you saw this?'

It's hard when you spend your whole life being an over-dramatic exaggerating storyteller because nobody believes you in real life when you are actually officially telling the real-life truth. This is what was happening now. I could tell.

'Yes!' I shout. 'Why would I lie?'

'Mum, she's not lying, I swear it. I saw it on here,' Poppy tries.

'I'm not saying either of you are lying. It's just, well, we have no proof, do we? If we can't find those photos.'

'Guess not,' I sigh.

'Yes, we can say we *saw* them,' Poppy pleads.

'Who is ever going to believe us now?' I huff.

'Don't worry about it, girls. Darcy, I will get Dad to phone in tomorrow and explain you've misplaced your book and could they please help hunt for it.' Mum goes to leave.

'*Misplaced? Misplaced?*' I heat up. Boiling anger rises. 'Mum, people *misplace* their umbrella, but this book is my whole entire *life*.'

'I know, I know, Darcy. Calm down – this is just to bring it to the school's attention. Now, let me put the shopping away.'

Up she gets, and I fold my arms and want to cry. It's like the world is cracking.

'Darcy?' Poppy asks. 'Is love still in the air or has it gone away now?'

Chapter Thirteen

The week lasts for ever. I am scared at every moment and cannot make sense of anything. I have so many questions swirling in my brain like:

1. Why did Jamie Haddock steal my book? Was it to trick me? To bribe me? To annoy or upset me? Was it to embarrass me? Maybe it was to write love stories about him and me in them and pretend I had written them?

2. Why did he put the pictures up on the internet? Why did he want everybody to know?

3. And, weirder . . . why did he take them down after only a few hours? Was he teasing me? What is he planning?

I live this week in constant fear of being shown up. I am taking Mum's advice of 'keeping a low profile', which means keep quiet and be as small as a mouse. I now know how celebrities feel when their whole lives get exposed in newspapers and everybody starts turning against them. I feel like I am walking on hot coals, waiting for that moment of getting burned.

Luckily for me, the teasing about my supposed romance with Jamie comes to an automatic halt because Alice Gates from the year below did a graffiti picture of a giant bum on the side of the dining hall and everybody was too busy being excited about that. Phew. But that doesn't bring my book back to me.

It's been nearly three weeks now since my writing book was stolen by Jamie Haddock and we have said nothing to each other. I don't dare talk to him becasue I'm worried that people will start the love rumours back up. School says they can't do or say anything to blame him for stealing my book because there is no 'evidence', and given my track record of mishaps with Jamie (punching him and throwing a rubber at his head) it's best if we 'let this one go'. I regret being nice to him for even one slither, but at least he is staying right out of my way, which is good. I was about to start using the writing book Will gave me anyway, so it's fine. The other one was all cracked and a bit broken and smelled of old smelly stuff. And it's like Dad says – *Nobody can take my stories away from my head or my heart*, which is extra-cheesy wheezy but true too. Writing must go on.

Chapter Fourteen

It's nearly Halloween, which is medium to extra-large amounts of OK. Weighing things up, this is what I've decided.

Halloween is good because:
1. I like sweets.
2. I like dressing up.
3. It's fun.
4. And you get to stay up late.

Halloween is not good because:
It's really scary.

We are not having a party because Mum has decided she can't be bothered with the 'hassle', and even when I begged her she still said no. It must be said that I'm not begging her the most I can beg, because I had a Halloween party once and I ended up smashing a clay lamp that came from a posh holiday Mum went on, then spilling lemonade onto the rug, and I do certainly not want her remembering that.

However, due to the fact that Donald is a spoiled brat from Bratland mixed in with a copycat, he knew we wanted a party at ours, and when his mum said no he cried and cried and stomped his feet and got his way and now the party is at the Pinchers' house. The Pinchers are richer than us, so maybe there will be more good things to eat. Then I remembered they don't have an imagination, and without an imagination what is the point of anything at all?

I have been thinking about this for days now. More days than could even exist.

What is the point of anything without an imagination?

Imagine when the world was just a world. I guess it began with cavemen. What would these cavemen and women have to work with? Stone? Rock? Sand? Nature? Animals? Everything would have had to come right from scratch, as they didn't have cookers or kettles or showers.

So people – walking, talking people like you and me – would have to think up all these amazing creations. They had to have ideas. Without ideas you are idea-less. And being idea-less means nothing. So think about what we have now – iPods, hairdryers and footbaths. These are all what my dad says are 'visions'.

I know these things take time. It's not as if the cavewoman was, like, 'Gosh, really, it's so annoying when I come out of washing in the river and my hair is wet, I really could do with a hairdryer.' It's not as simple as that; these things take time. But without somebody thinking it up in the first place . . . well . . . it wouldn't exist, would it?

Anyway.

It isn't long before it's time to stop thinking about that and have a think about our costumes. Already Poppy is going as a ghost and Hector is going as a zombie snake. He was *supposed* to just be a zombie, but he is into snakes too at the moment. I guess I was fine with this, but it needed a back story, so the character background is: *He's a snake back from the dead to seek revenge on a mean zoo-keeper who didn't feed him any mouses, I mean mice, for so long he died and now he's back to haunt him.*

'Let me thicken this plot up a bit,' I laugh to Hector, as I peel open the first new page of my writing book. I am glad I am doing this with him, otherwise I would be thinking about my lost book far too much.

The Zombie Snake

It had been so long since the snake had been
fed. For weeks he had suffered; imagining the
stupid penguins swallowing their flapping fishes,
the lion with his chunks of bloody steak, the
giraffes slowly munching the leaves and treats
from a tall tree.

But here, under the green shadowy light
of the reptile centre, he had to watch the
tarantulas attacking their prey and the googly-
eyed lizards waiting for their moment to strike
at their victims, all believing that they were
actually out in the wild.

What had he done to that pig of a
zoo-keeper to make him so furious as to not
feed him? It didn't matter now as he felt his
heartbeat slowing to a stillness: all he wanted
was his revenge.

'That sounds wicked.' Hector clapped when I had finished reading it out to him. 'And what do snakes even eat anyway?'

'Mice.'

'Mouses?' he asks.

'Yes.'

'Yuck.' He pokes his tongue out. 'Can you read it again?' and so I do.

I've been racking my brainbox thinking about what to be for Halloween, but Mum's ideas are all so dry. Like witch and vampire and all of those – so boring. Mum thinks that now I'm 'just being difficult', and even when I say 'I'm not' she says I am. And I know it's because I reckon this party will not be fantastic. I bet there won't be any eyeballs floating in the punch; bet there won't even *be* any punch. Bet there will be no severed old ladies' fingers, no gut jelly, no apple bobbing, no pin-the-screw-on-the-Frankenstein, no toffee apples.

Later on, Mum and Dad are having a big mahoosive, stupid fight about Halloween:

ACT 1, SCENE 1

Stage curtain up. Kitchen. Early evening. Mum is writing a shopping list. Dad is making dinner. Something beginning with lots of onions.

The debate: Should we still have a pumpkin?

Mum Yes, of course we should. It's Halloween, the kids like it and everybody else on the road will have one.

Dad It's an effort, they are a fire hazard and it's a mess to carve.

Mum We can make pumpkin soup.

Dad You say that every year and you never make it.

Mum You really just don't want a pumpkin because they are heavy to carry.

Dad Yes, that as well.

Mum tuts and shakes her head, which she is very skilled at doing, and Dad sighs helplessly, which means Mum has won. Curtain down. End of Act.

197

Or something like that. This goes on for a while before Mum is already drawing some designs on paper about what face to give our pumpkin, even though really all she needs to do is arrange a creative meeting with me and I will be more than happy to assist her with what I have up my sleeve. Which are basically some good ideas on how to carve the pumpkin.

And then this one starts:

ACT 1, SCENE 2

Stage curtain up. Kitchen, early evening, about one second after Scene 1.

The debate: Do we get sweets for the other kids for trickle treating?

Mum Yes, of course we do. When kids knock, they want sweets, and we can't just give them nothing.

Dad We won't give them *nothing.* I just

don't want to spend a small fortune on Jelly Tots for a load of nuisance kids knocking when they should be tucked up in bed.

Mum A small fortune? We are talking about a few lollipops and some Maltesers, not a trip to the Caribbean. When did you become such a Scrooge anyway? What are you planning on giving these kids then when they knock?

Dad Well, I'm sure we will have some . . . bread knocking about?

Mum Bread? *Bread?*

Dad Yes, bread.

Mum So thirty kids show up at the door, dressed up, looking brilliant, and you reward them with bread?

Dad It's better for them, and it will keep them going in the cold night.

Mum They are not *beggars*.

Dad You're ridiculous.

Mum You're outrageous. Perhaps I'll pop
down to the local garden shop and get
a birdbath for them too, since you must
think these children have the appetite of
small birds.

Dad laughs.

Dad Fine, well, get what you want, but you
shouldn't be encouraging children to knock
on strangers' doors.

Mum It's HALLOWEEN!

Dad Well, I just won't answer the door all
night.

Curtain down. End of Act.

Is it Trickle Treating or Trick or Treating? I am
not sure.

Our pumpkin has a wonky eye, but other than
that he is good and he has candles in his body.
Obviously we made no pumpkin soup because it

was so seedy and we couldn't be bothered.

I am going to the Halloween party as the spider in my room. Mum has rummaged through her drawers and rescued four pairs of old black tights and we have stuffed these with newspaper for my legs. A spider is quite a good idea.

Lamb-Beth has some red devil ears on and a red cape. She looks cute.

Mum hasn't come in the end because she has decided she wants to have a bubble bath and close her eyes. Boring.

We turn up at the Pinchers' house and Dad is telling me to cheer up and not to judge and not to be mean and think happy thoughts, and then he goes stricter and says if I'm not nice I won't even get to see the party at all, and me and Lamb-Beth 'will be in the car on our way home before we can say BOO!' *Well, good,* I think.

Already I am jealous because their pumpkin is actually fabulous. It is mahoosive, with big scary eyes and a gaping open mouth with a giant puddle of mushed-up pumpkin pouring out of its mouth as if the pumpkin had been sick. Gross and mixed in with amazing. I just don't know which one of the Pinchers was imaginative enough to think up that idea – it seems unlikely that it could have been any of them.

Marnie opens the door and does that high-pitched squeal she always does which could crack a tea set.

'Welcome to the House of Horrors!' she warbles and I think to myself how annoying, but actually she is quite brilliantly scary-looking. She is dressed as a Victorian maid. But I think she's trying to be a little too sexy for my liking. She is holding a feather duster and she tickles my cheek with it.

'I love your costume, Darcy. What are you? An ant?'

'A spider.'

'Oh, of course you are.' And then she pulls me into the House of Horrors and sings the entirety of 'Incy Wincy Spider' at me. Which is actually, to be honest, really destroying my menacing look.

Suddenly it all becomes very frightening. The dark hallways are draped with skull-shaped lights, there's stringy cobwebby fluff decorating the corners of the living room and a flashing floodlight that crackles and cackles every twenty seconds to make it look like there is a thunderstorm inside the house. Outside in real life it has started to rumble thunder too, and the rain sounds like skeleton fingers against the windows.

I start to feel worried and scared for Mum indoors all by herself in the bath with her eyes closed, listening to the frightening thunderstorm outside.

It's difficult at Halloween because you never know who is who; it's so easy to suddenly become a stranger when you're disguised. This is what frightens me the most, I think, as I turn sideways to enter the sitting room where the party is, so that all of my eight legs can get through safely. I worry that I will not be able to tell who people are under their masks.

It turns out that it is actually not all that hard to figure out who is who because there are only about eight of us here.

Donald has come as that bad Uncle Fester from

The Addams Family and he has on a rubbery fake bald head. Mainly it looks stupid as it's too tanned for his skin, but his make-up is really good. Marnie must have done it.

'Darcy has come as a spider. Doesn't she look just fantastic, Donald?' Marnie rattles.

'Thought you were a flea,' Donald chuckles to himself.

I scowl at him as dramatically as I can before Dad catches my eye, and so I pretend I am intensely interested in John Pincher, who has come as a scary ringleader from a circus. He has on fantastic shoes with curly toe bits but he is annoying everybody because he keeps shouting 'Roll up, roll up!' and I don't think anybody much feels like *rolling up* anywhere.

The food table is actually quite spectacular and everything has a little hand-made sign next to it saying what it's supposed to be: ginormous bowls of Monster Munch feet, trays of curly fries with *Witches' Fingers* written beside them, plates of jam tarts marked

Blood Tarts, and a massive pan of yummy macaroni cheese that smells amazing and has a sign next to it saying *Maggots in Pus*. Eurgh. Who thought that up? Must have been Donald. I feel a bit sick after reading that.

The table has been decorated so good. A big steaming lamp is setting an amazing smoky effect all over the table so it looks like a massive fog is hanging over us. Tangles and tangles of fake cobwebs and fake skeleton bones hang all over the spread, nudged in between a scattering of delicious toffee apples and pyramid-shaped sugary sweets.

Yum, yum, yum and yum again.

Dad shoots me a look over the room that is all 'I told you so', and I feel like losing my mind at him a bit, but he was right. This is fun.

When we hear that the rain stops, we know we can have fireworks outside. Dad and John do all the scary bits with the lighters, sparking the end of the rockets and then running away to be safe, whilst us kids watch from the living-room window, all piled in the warmth waiting for the sky to explode into a fiery rainbow.

PSSSSSSSSHHHHHH pink purple CRACK turquoise silver WHHHHHHAAAAAAA gold blue RAAAAHHHHH FIZZZZZZZZZZZZZZ glitter red CRACK orange yellow CRACKLE SSSHHH-HHHHHHHHHHH the night-black sky.

Afterwards we draw words with sparklers. I write 'Darcy' and 'Lamb-Beth' and 'Mum' and try to do 'Magnificent', but I don't know how to spell

'Magnificent' so I am glad sparkler ink doesn't last for ever. I take so many pictures with my eyes, so that when I close them I can see my words in silvery glittery lines.

We pile back into the kitchen and then out come the most floppy scrumptious pancakes. Mrs Pincher has made tons of them, all racked up like stacks of squashed beach balls, steam rising out of the top, ready to be drenched in sugar and lemon. Reaching for the warm plates, we grab stacks of pancakes, taking turns in passing round the sugar pot, gently scattering the sweet white dust over our pancakes, squeezing the lemon, letting the sour juice pour over the sweetness and allowing the warmth of the pancake to begin to cook the lemony flavour, making the most scrumptious smell. Poppy is complaining a bit, because her finger is still sore from where she sharpened it and the lemon juice is irritating it. But Dad squeezes her lemon for her and wraps her finger in a tissue.

'Look, it's like your finger is an Egyptian mummy now,' he laughs, and sticks two little Monster Munch crumbs on top for eyes.

'Cool.' Hector smiles. And then we all gobble up our pancakes, missing Mum a bit, but still gobbling.

'Does anybody know the horror pancake house story?' John Pincher interrupts the gobbling.

'No,' I say.

'Don't tell it, John, the kids will be terrified!' Mrs Pincher hoots and John Pincher rolls his eyeballs as if to say, *It's just a story*.

'Yeah, Darcy will wet the bed if she hears that one!' Donald adds in between scoffs. *Shut up, Donald*.

'No, I won't,' I defend myself.

'Darcy loves stories,' Dad says, sticking up for me. 'We all do. I'm sure we will be fine.'

'Yes,' I say. 'I'm sure we *will* be fine. Thank you very much anyway, but it's just a story.'

'Hmmmm . . . or so they say . . .' John Pincher grizzles so slyly like a sneaky actor, and then he does a big old belly laugh that rumbles the room so loud and then he begins . . .

'*The Misery of the Pancake House*.

'Mr Ridley is going for a job interview. He is going

for a job interview at a very posh important office in the centre of London,' John says, wiping his chin and getting comfy.

'What job was he doing?' Poppy asks curiously, gnawing around the side of a toffee apple and then taking another bite of her pancake.

'Something important.'

'Yeah, like what?'

'Like a businessman sort of job.'

'Like a newsreader?'

'Hm. No. Not on television.'

'Oh, so like a teacher.'

'Not exactly.'

'Oh . . . so . . . like a dad?'

'Well, no, a businessman, so a posh . . . Don't worry too much about it, Poppy.' Mr Pincher sighs, already fed up, has a glug of fizzy beer and continues, 'He is excited about this job interview because he knows that on either side of the office where his new job could be are two wonderful shops. One is a tie shop, and Mr Ridley loves ties. He has a collection of three hundred and nineteen at home and has plenty of room for more. And the other shop is a pancake house, and Mr Ridley also loves pancakes. He especially loves this particular pancake house because it has every type of pancake with every type of pancake filling you could ever wish up. Like ham and cheese, cheese and pickle, jam and cheese, sausage and bacon, sugar and lemon—'

'We had sugar and lemon pancakes!' Poppy shouts, which makes everybody jump a bit because we have been so silent for so long.

'Poppy, be quiet and let John tell us what happened,' Dad says.

'Let me tell this blooming thing, will you?' John huffs. 'Where were we? Ah yes, pancake fillings, so salami and tomato, banana and Nutella, chicken curry, red cabbage and artichoke, spaghetti and meatballs, fried egg and custard (that is a weird one, yes, but believe me, it sells) and then Mr Ridley's real favourite – the *Secret Special Pancake flavour*.

'On the Tube, on his way to his job interview in

the centre of London in the very posh important office, Mr Ridley transports his mind away from all the nerves he is feeling about his interview and lets his mind gently sway towards something positive, and there was nothing more positively mind-swaying than the mouth-watering offerings of the glorious ingredients in the *Secret Special Pancake* pancake. He thinks about it for a very long time, so much he nearly dribbles down his novelty yellow spotty tie and misses his train stop.

'Mr Ridley is most pleased when he arrives at the large revolving door of the office and sees, to the right, the tie shop and, to the left the pancake house. How it would really suit him working here, he thinks, how he would really take to working here like a duck to water, like a cactus to the desert, like a fried egg to custard.

'Mr Ridley's job interview goes absolutely swimmingly and lots of friendly chatter goes on about Mr Ridley's interest in travelling and fine wine and especially his love of ties. And Mr Ridley was offered a job right there on the spot and was even offered a chocolate digestive and a cup of coffee to celebrate. "But no thanks," said Mr Ridley. "I am saving my appetite. I'm going to get a pancake from the pancake house next door."'

John put on a voice for the woman boss, which was funny and girlie and high-pitched.

"'What?" his new boss asked darkly. "Really?"'

"'Oh yes, I like it there very much." Mr Ridley hummed.

"'You've eaten there before?" His new boss looked very nervous now, and a little speckly rash began creeping up her throat like a strangling clawing hand.

"'Yes, often, I find it absolutely delicious."'

"'Have you tried the Italian round the corner?" his new boss tried to persuade him. "Honestly, they do the most wonderful carbonara."'

"'I'm quite happy with the pancake house," grinned Mr Ridley.

"'What about the Spanish? It truly is the real deal

– fantastic tapas, and it's not expensive either."

"'No, really, I have been looking forward to my pancake." Mr Ridley patted his belly and sighed. Mr Ridley was such an open-faced and harmless man with excellent morals and a kind inoffensive smile that suddenly melted away the awkwardness of the moment.

"'All right . . . well . . . enjoy."

"'Cheerio! See you Monday." Mr Ridley grinned, glowing.

"'Yes . . ." His new boss waved him off, and her eyes gazed over Mr Ridley for a little too long. What a nice man he was and what a shame.'

'What was a shame?' Poppy butts it.

'Poppy, let John tell the story.' I squeezed her hand, but not the pencil-sharpened one.

John begins again. 'The smell of the pancake house was exactly as Mr Ridley had remembered it, warm and buttery, eggy and sugary, homely and fattening.

"'Good morning, sir, how are you?" smiled the

large ruddy-faced lady behind the counter.

"'Very good indeed, thank you for asking, I have just got myself a new job.'"

"'Bravo!'" clapped the woman. "'Where is your new job?'"

"'Why thank you!'" laughed Mr Ridley. "'Just next door.'"

"'Oh, in the very posh offices?'" The woman nosed over and flared her nostrils; they fanned out like the nose of a dragon.

"'Yes. Then I will be able to come to the pancake house every day!'" He smiled, ordered his *Secret Special Pancake* and chose a table in the corner of the quaint little restaurant. Mr Ridley was so proud of himself he could have given himself a cuddle. Just to think, only this morning he was lying in bed with absolutely nothing, and here he was having a lovely lunch at the pancake house with a brand-new job in a very posh, important office to look forward to.

"'*Secret Special!*'" called the large piggy-nosed woman from behind the counter, even though she knew that Mr Ridley was the only customer there. Here it was, his pancake; his meaty, smoky, saucy, spicy, herby, tangy, drippy, cheesy, gooey, chunky, melty, sloppy, tasty, no wasty pancake, and every bite was terrific.

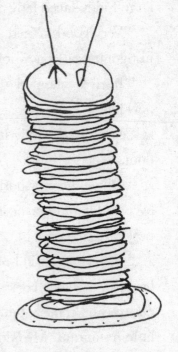

'When he finished, he wiped his mouth very politely with a napkin and then he smiled contently, full and happy, at the lady behind the counter.

'"What is in that *Secret Special Pancake* that makes it *so* secret and *so* special? If only I knew," he beamed, "I would die a happy man." And then he collapsed.

His head fell onto his plate with a splodgy stodgy splat, his eyes started and crazed, his jaw twisted at an angle.'

'What happened?' Poppy screamed.

'If you shut up you will find out!' Donald roared.

'Don't tell Poppy to *shut up*,' I roared back.

'I'll tell *you* to *shut up* instead then. Shut up.'

'Kids . . .' Dad hissed. Which means, in Dad language, *Stop it*. So we do. I bring Lamb-Beth close. John Pincher continues with his story.

'When the lady that worked behind the counter at the pancake shop saw Mr Ridley collapse into his empty pancake-splattered plate, she did not call an ambulance, she did not panic, she did not collapse or throw a glass of cold water over his head, she did not run out in the street and ask for help, she did not make a fuss, she did not stand startled and confused or try and wake him up. Nope, she simply went over to the front door, locked it and spun the sign on the door round from OPEN to CLOSED.'

Suddenly this story was getting very scary. I could feel my hands getting very sweaty. My imagination, you see, is like losing a receipt in the wind. Once it flies away it will tease you endlessly, swirling and

forever making itself impossible to grasp, never for one moment stopping still.

'It is rather gruesome and pretty gross to say what exactly happened to Mr Ridley in the kitchen at the pancake house. But you must know that the brittle clunking that sounded similar to the chopping of a tree, as the special filling was wrapped in scrambled

eggs, could be heard by the neighbours. Passers-by couldn't help but notice the blood flecks splattered on the pancake house window. *Just sauce*, some would say. *Must just be sauce.*'

'Poor Mr Ridley!' Poppy shouted, and then clamped her hands over her mouth when everybody chorused *'Shhhhhhhhhhhhhhhh!'*

'A week later, Mr Ball, another man, was very excited. He was very excited because he had just gone and got himself a new job – what a clog of cleverness! He left the office under the warm umbrella of sunshine, letting his head bathe in the warm spring air.

'"Hmmm," he grinned, briefcase swinging. "I fancy treating myself to a bite to eat." He pushed open the door of the pancake house, taking in the warm, buttery, eggy, sugary, homely and fattening smell and the little hand-made sign that said: *Try our Secret Special Pancake, containing fresh homemade ingredients*. And thinking to himself, *How wonderful, I wonder what that secret special ingredient is*.'

'What happened?' Poppy asked.

'Mr Ridley ended up being put in a pancake,' I gasped.

'What? How?'

'He was the secret ingredient,' I said.

Poppy gulped. 'You mean . . . that new man . . . Mr Ball . . . he ate him?'

'Yes.' I felt a bit sick.

'And it makes you wonder, what do you think the secret ingredient was in Mr *Ridley*'s pancake?' Dad asked us.

'Eugh! Gross!'

'That's so naughty,' Hector decides.

'So stupid, is what it is,' Donald humphs. 'It's silly and dumb and unrealistic. I used to, like, listen to that story when I was, like, one and I still wasn't scared.'

'Bet you were,' I say softly, as though I can somehow trespass into the kind part of his heart and he will, for once, be nice.

'No way,' he snorts. 'Cannibals don't scare me one bit.'

I bet he was scared, I think to myself, and then to make myself feel better I eat maybe nearly a bajillion chocolate buttons.

After apple bobbing, Hector the zombie snake has fallen asleep and Poppy has white face make-up in her eyes and they are red and stinging, so Dad suggests we go home.

'How was the party?' Mum asks. She looks so peaceful and relaxed, as though she has been at a spa for a zillion years, and we all look a mess.

I am trying to drag bedtime out as much as I

can but eventually it is time to surrender. I am not scared or anything, but I just feel like the hour feels so itchy and uncomfy, it's like I have a stone in my shoe that I can't shake out. Later on, in bed, I am sweaty and my heart won't relax down to a normal drumbeat. I feel so afraid. I can't even breathe or move or think about anything else other than the smell of pancakes and the horrible story that John told us.

Then I start thinking about the pancakes we ate at the Pinchers'. *Oh, what if I ated a human being person by accident hidden in pancake batter? Oh no!* I wonder if Poppy is this frightened in her bed? I am tossing and turning and keep wanting the light to be switched back on, but I am too scared to get out from underneath the covers and put my feet on the floor in case the pancake house has sent a representative to hide under my bed and snap me up and turn me into pancake filling. And then I realize that I am so scared and the bedroom feels so big and every shape and shadow looks like claws coming to get me and ginormous pancakes are falling from the ceiling to swallow me up and axes coming down to hack me up, and I am afraid but I don't want to scream for my dad because then he will know that after all I am scared of scary stories.

So I open up my writing book.

With so many worries and over-worrying about worrying, it simply is a wonder how sometimes I even manage to get to sleep. Do mums and dads and teachers and nurses and policeman still get horror dreams too? Some days I imagine myself being a grandma and still getting awful night frights about the silliest things. Plus maybe it's worserer when you're older anyway, because on top of the scares you have about ghosts and monsters and vampires, you also have to worry about money and arguments and the terrible things you read in the newspapers.

Screaming Gloria and Edward Vinegar

Gloria was not in any sort of state of *glory*,

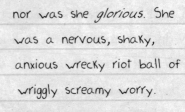

nor was she *glorious*. She was a nervous, shaky, anxious wrecky riot ball of wriggly screamy worry.

If Gloria was waiting for the toaster to finish toasting her crumpets and it popped up, even if she was waiting for the 'ping', she would scream.

If Gloria was at home and the telephone rang unexpectedly or not, she would scream.

If Gloria switched on the light in her own bedroom, and I mean if *she* actually switched on the light in *her very own bedroom*, she would indeed scream, purely from seeing the room go from darkness to light.

I know what you must be thinking: *How utterly exhausting*. And you are right – what an utterly exhausting existence.

The reason Gloria was so nervy and jumpy and screamy was very simple. She was absolutely terrified of absolutely everything.

Getting herself up and ready for a trip to the supermarket was noisy and jumpy, and leaving the house was even worse, full of panic and terror for fear of hearing a dog bark near her or a flock of pigeons spontaneously flap off in flight. But she needed to go every day at exactly the same time of 11 a.m. sharp; otherwise, she believed something could go terribly wrong. The staff were used to her, and so were the townspeople. They nicknamed her 'Screaming Gloria'.

One day she was teetering around the tins section in aisle seven for chicken soup when an unexpected turn for the worse happened . . .

A tin of soup fell from the shelf.

To anybody else this would sound like this:

Bang.

To Gloria it sounded like what you would hear if the world had popped like a giant water balloon, as though the earth was ripping from the core of the universe inside out, CRASHING, RIPPING, TEARING, EXPLODING, and so naturally, obviously, she screamed: 'AHHHHRAHHHHHHHHHHHHHH!'

Of course, this behaviour was very normal from Screaming Gloria, and the other supermarket locals were used to it, so after her heartbeat had relaxed to its normal rapid rate Gloria continued shopping for chicken soup, milk, eggs, coconut rings . . .

But somebody who was very sneaky and very sly, somebody very clever and very smart, somebody who was very witty and very observant saw an opportunity they were not about to throw away.

Edward Vinegar was a very poor man – he was like real poor. Like Gloria, Edward Vinegar had a very similar routine at supermarket time, which is also 11 a.m. Edward's supermarket visiting time is 11 a.m. because it is the changing of the security guard hour.

I'm not sure if you've ever seen the changing of the guards in a supermarket, but for those who haven't, it goes a bit like this:

'All right, mate?'

'Yeah, you?'

'Not bad, mate, not bad.'

'Up to much?'

'No, not really, mate. You?'

'Nah, not really.'

This distracting and ever-so-boring conversation gives Edward Vinegar a five-minute window to steal, vigorously, and so he does. Daily. He steals anything he can: tea bags, jars of jam, bagels, yoghurt, cream tarts, chocolate bars – you name it, he steals it. Every day he spies this fumbling nervous Gloria and he laughs at her and thinks, *What a nervous mess of a woman.* But he never once goes to help her when she is scared or anxious or worried.

Today he is in the supermarket shoplifting corn flakes and loaves of bread when he, as usual, notices the very nervy Gloria and his mind spins into a whirlwind of special clever ideas.

He leaves the shop, rubbing his moustache in crafty menace.

That night he went to his tiny scraggy little bedsit and, being the burrower that he was, scavenged through his collection of junk and found a small glass cylinder. 'Perfect,' he sniggered to himself.

Next, in a big jug, Edward Vinegar mixed up a very clever concoction of lots

and lots and lots and plenty of cold tea. He
stirred up the mixture very quickly, adding water
to loosen it as he went, until it formed a fine
light brown liquid. He decanted the fluid into
the glass cylinder.

Next he had to label his cylinder. He wanted
this cylinder to look as authentic as possible.
Edward Vinegar hadn't anything fancy like a
computer or any posh pens, but he did have
a fine collection of second-hand books. So he
carefully found all the letters he needed to label
his cylinder, and then, as neatly as he most
possibly could, cut out using scissors the letters
from the pages in the second-hand book until
he had all the letters for the word he needed.
With a blob of man-made glue (a handful
of flour and some water), he very delicately
positioned each letter onto the cylinder using a
pair of tweezers from a lady's manicure set he
had rescued from a skip.

He puzzled his word together and dried the

wet glue by blowing on each letter. *Well, I'm rather pleased with that*, he thought to himself as he popped it into the fridge to chill. He then celebrated his brainwave in style, with a giant bowl of corn flakes.

The next morning Edward Vinegar was on a level of excitement that made him feel like his feet had jelly in them and his tummy had cherryade in. He brushed himself up the very best he ever could, propped his hat at an attractive charming angle and practised his sales pitch. He felt so pleased with himself and so smart and so sharp.

And at a quarter to eleven it seemed the perfect time to toddle down to the supermarket and bump into the nervous wreck otherwise known as 'Screaming Gloria'.

It wasn't long before he saw her, pawing her hand over a basket of plums, terrified that at any moment a creepy crawly would scuttle out from in between the fruit and prick her hand with its pincers.

Edward Vinegar seized his chance.

'Good morning,' he charmed brightly over the pineapples.

'Morning,' Gloria mumbled. (Speaking to strangers, of course, was an absolute no-no.)

'Please don't be afraid. Allow me to

introduce myself as Doctor Edward Vinegar, as in Balsamic, not Malt.' He laughed, all spitty between the teeth.

'Is that your *real* name?' Gloria asked, her eyes shifting to the ground.

'Of course it is.' Edward Vinegar tried not to let the comment offend him and carried on in character.

'You don't look like much of a doctor.' Gloria shuffled, eyeing up Edward Vinegar's browning cords and rotting dull grey jumper.

'*Inventor*, I prefer,' he beamed. 'Besides, how many inventors have you ever come across before?'

Gloria thought, *Not many. In fact, none at all.*

Edward Vinegar pushed again. 'I am just doing a bit of showcasing, launching my new invention, just trying to meet a few friendly faces and show them my . . . errr . . . *remedies.*'

'Remedies?'

'Yes, I am an expert at making people confident.'

At this, Gloria stood amazed. The word gave her the bumpy lumps. 'Confidence?' she questioned him quickly. 'But how?'

'It's very simple. It is quite simply a wonderful medicine to make you not jumpy or squirmy or worried or nervous or prickly or afraid.'

'But how?' Gloria worried. She didn't like to take any medicine at all, because she had heard terrifying stories about what could happen if you took too much or too little.

Edward Vinegar was a bit worried too; what if Screaming Gloria laughed in his face or called his bluff? So much relied on his sales pitch, and what if it crumbled into a mess of nothing?

But then he thought to himself, *I can't sell bottled confidence if I am not confident myself!* And with that he produced the little glass cylinder from his pocket.

'Four drops of this, four times a day.'

Gloria inspected the bottle. She had her doubts, but a life without worry would be a life worth having. She could go to the beach, the zoo, Top Shop, on holiday, to the nail salon, maybe even have a little glass of champagne and read her book in a fancy cocktail bar? Oh, life would be bliss and, surprising herself, she whispered, 'How much?'

This was the bit, the scary bit. Edward Vinegar had to be strong and believe in his price. He had read somewhere two things:

1. That you should overvalue yourself and

your products always, even if they are a
load of old rubbish.
2. That ninety-nine pounds sounds much
   cheaper than one hundred pounds, even
   though it is only a small pound less.

'Ninety-nine pounds,' he said proudly.

Wowza matrowzer. Ninety-nine pounds was
an awful lot of money: it could buy lots of
chicken soup and plums, it could buy tea bags
and wool slippers, but Gloria had to be honest
with herself; she couldn't put a price on
confidence.

'I'll take it.'

And Edward Vinegar, as much as he
wanted to squeal over and kiss Screaming
Gloria a trillion times, he could not, he had to
stay smart and sophisticated and professional,
as though he did these kinds of deals all
the time. So he nodded casually, and said
something snobby like, 'Wise choice.' And took

her money and handed her the bottle.

Edward Vinegar snuck away as quick as a rabbit. He had to move fast before Screaming Gloria realized her bottle of 'Confidence' was nothing more than a cylinder of cold tea. *But first*, he thought, *a new pair of socks would do nicely.*

Now this was just getting silly. Gloria was sat at home, scared to take the confidence drops she had just paid all that money for, but she knew she had to try them, for how else would she become as fearless as a dragon?

'Here goes,' she muttered, as she twisted off the cap of the glass cylinder and, using the pipette, released four single droplets onto her tongue.

'Tastes like tea,' she mumbled, surprised, letting the cold liquid fill her mouth and then calmly folding her hands onto her lap and waiting for the effects.

236

Now, reader, I do not want to lie to you here and pretend this story is not like those other stories where people trick others into believing what they are doing/taking/drinking/eating/seeing is the real McCoy when in fact it is not. Because it is. It is definitely one of those stories. As we all know, Edward Vinegar put nothing but cold black tea into a glass cylinder and sold it to poor Gloria for nearly one hundred pounds. Which is wrong. But this story is a little different, because in this story something even more peculiar happens.

This bottled confidence didn't just make Gloria think she was confident, it made Gloria believe she was a superhero. A superhero who could do anything.

She flung all the windows open, letting the cool breeze charge into the house, which she never does for fear of a burglar. She baked a cake, which she never does for fear of burning the house down. She put on make-up, which she never does for fear of an allergic reaction. She put her hair up into a high ponytail, which she never does for fear of pulling her face off. She put on high heels, which she never does for fear of tripping up and breaking her ankle or getting the heel caught in a drain. And out she tottered, waving at people on the street, saying, 'Hi,' petting dogs and only stopping once to have four more droplets of bottled confidence.

Wow! she thought. *This stuff is terrific.*

Little did she know the only medication she was having was four droplets of cold old tea.

After buying his new socks (and a few other things), Edward Vinegar was feeling pretty darn special, but he had to make a move – it would not be long before Screaming Gloria realized she had been tricked and would angrily be wanting a refund. As he stood on the street corner, hitchhiking for a car to take him to the station, he saw Gloria dressed up like a Barbie doll,

strutting down the high street, and before he could hide she caught his eye and ran over.

'Thank you so much!' she said. 'Look at me, I feel amazing. The bottled confidence is working brilliantly!' She beamed at Edward Vinegar enormously.

And it wasn't long before Edward's heart was beating, and all he was noticing was that actually Gloria was quite wonderful and quite pretty and a little bit funny and a little bit quirky and interesting, and as soon as he was about to think to himself, *I quite fancy this woman*, Gloria blurted out of her new confident mouth, 'Would you please like to take me for dinner?'

And Edward Vinegar said, 'Yes.'

Edward Vinegar and Screaming Gloria were having a lovely time, Gloria's confidence was rocket-sky-soaring-high and Edward Vinegar got himself a job as an estate agent, which was an absolutely perfect job for him. And of course he was still secretly making up Gloria's bottled confidence, but not charging her *quite so much* and still never revealing the very simple and very dishonest ingredient.

Gloria was so confident now there was nothing she couldn't do. She had taken up tightrope-walking classes, juggling courses, was a regular at the local karaoke bar (singing anything by Adele); she wore knee-high sparkly pink boots, she cut all her hair off and dyed it blue, she got a lip piercing, she took German lessons, she entered a pottery-making competition and did a bungee-jump. Making up for lost time or what?

However, when anybody first met Gloria she was so talkative and chatty and funny and interesting that nobody seemed to notice Edward. It was as though he was being rubbed out by a big fat Gloria-shaped rubber. All he would hear was, 'Where's Gloria?' and 'Bring Gloria along.' Or, 'Gloria is so great.' And after a time it was as though people wanted to spend more time with her than they did with him.

And everything that Edward thought he could do – Gloria could do better.

She was better at talking, reading, making friends, writing, cooking, cleaning, dancing, singing, making crafts, jumping, driving, riding a bike and being a person.

And after some time, Edward's confidence began to shrivel away and disappear.

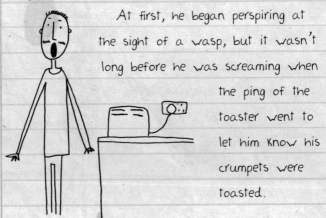

At first, he began perspiring at the sight of a wasp, but it wasn't long before he was screaming when the ping of the toaster went to let him know his crumpets were toasted.

Gloria's newfound confidence had stolen his.

Edward's personality evaporated, like the last flecks from a winter snowman in the sun. He was weak. He tried to make himself some 'bottled confidence', but it didn't work, for he knew it was nothing but old brown, cold tea.

He needed to explain what he had done to Gloria, he had to come clean, but she was always too busy attending film premieres and going to five-star restaurants with comedians to listen to Edward. He had, indeed, created a monster.

Here is Edward today, shivering in his chair, too scared to even flick the TV on for fear of it exploding. Waiting for Gloria to come home from the stars.

Hmmm. That story was quite *grown up*, I think to myself as I close my new writing book. I am no longer scared of the horror pancake house.

Chapter Fifteen

Poppy has an audition at a dance school tomorrow. She has shown me her dance. It is her version of a Fred Astaire piece. You are probably thinking, *Who on earth is this Fred Astaire chap?* And I am not surprised, as nobody in my life knows who he is either, other than Mum and Dad and Henrietta. He basically is an old dancer from way back, even in black-and-white TV times! He was the best dancer ever, even way better than Justin or Usher, and he used to hang out with this most beautiful lady called Ginger Rogers, who has big blue eyes and fur coats. You should YouTube them for sure.

Anyway, he is Poppy's favourite dancer in the

kingdom. Mum suggested maybe something a little more 'current', but what does she know? Plus it really suits my sister.

We are all excited the night before, because if Poppy gets in she will be doing dancing all day, every day, like ballet and tap and hip-hop and even country line dancing.

Mum is just finishing the final touches to her costume, which is a sparkly cowgirl suit. It's so cool,

with a fake cow-skin hat, and she even has a water pistol that she sprays at the judges when the song finishes.

We watch her rehearse one more time before bed, with mugs of hot milk, and Dad is so proud and says, 'I really hope you get this, Pops.'

Me as well.

In bed later I can imagine all of Poppy's life as an excellent dancer: filling every seat in the biggest theatres, getting in and out of posh limos and receiving flowers every night from hot actors that have seen her face in *Vogue* and want to take her to eat oysters.

What do oysters taste like? I wonder, as I drift off to sleep.

The next morning is mayhem manic mania. Hector has banged his head on the bath because he was crying so hard about not wanting to wash his hair and started screaming like a mental person in a mental hospital. Mum is plaiting Poppy's hair into excellent cowgirl plaits and Dad's making breakfast

– dippy egg, but it isn't a birthday and even though Mum agrees that Poppy needs a hearty breakfast before her audition, she also says that 'egg is so time-consuming'.

But I love egg.

Finally, when it's time to go, we pile into the car and I have to leave Lamb-Beth at home, but it's OK because it's not raining so she has the whole garden to roam around in and graze on the grass.

Poppy looks *so* cool. She is going to blow every-body's minds.

The dance school is in a posh area and it takes ages to drive there, but I love sitting in the back seat and listening to Dad's old punk music and looking out of the window. Especially in the posherest areas where all those women walk around with takeaway coffee cups and clippy-cloppy shoes and ginormous, glamorous handbags, yacky-yack-yacking on their phones.

We are late. But we are always late so I don't know so much what the fuss is all about, but Mum is nearly being about to have a heart attack and she is beating her hand so fast on the dashboard and vibrating so much it's like she's a bottle of fizzy water about to explode.

She says to Dad, 'I'm going to have to run Poppy in. You'll have to park the car.'

Dad nods and quickly checks the address of the dance school with Mum. 'Good luck, Poppy!' he shouts out the window.

'What if we miss her, Dad?' I panic as we drive into the dark dingy concrete car park.

'We won't.'

'But we might.'

'We won't.' Dad concentrates on driving and I concentrate on not missing Poppy's audition.

Dad, Hector and I run-run-rabbit-run as quick as we can into the dance-school doors which flap open shut and then open. *You could really catch a finger in there*, I'm thinking as we head to the reception desk.

'Hi, we are here for the auditions,' my dad pants breathlessly.

RECEPTION

'Oh. Right. You are late.' The receptionist is what Mum would call 'a cow'. And I'm already knowing that I hate it here. Then she adds, 'Through the double doors, up the first flight of stairs, you will see a large clock, something that perhaps *you* should invest in . . .' This weird comment passes over my head like an aeroplane, but I can tell it's rude because Dad does a snort. She continues, 'Left there, through the next set of double doors, take a sharp right, down the long corridor, up round the spiral staircase, right to the top, through the giant arch and then through the door with the brass handle.'

She smiles shortly and goes back to her paper-work. Which I obviously bet is really just a stupid crossword puzzle.

I gasp widely at Dad. This is what Frodo must have felt like in *Lord of the Rings* when he has to go on that looooooooonnnnggggg trek to dump that well-annoying ring.

The walk is not too bad because there are loads of funny photographs all over the walls of girls the same age as me doing dancing and taking themselves really seriously and making faces like they are having a big poo. Dad is laughing too.

The floors are all shiny marble, which is fun for swishing but Dad tells me off and says I 'have to behave' and reminds me that 'today is a big day for Poppy'. So I pretend to be posh instead. Dad laughs at me and calls me 'Her Majesty' and 'Darlinnnnggg' in a fake French accent.

We are the only late ones, I think.

We get in and the auditions have

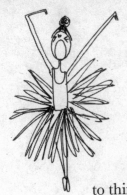

only just started so I really don't know what that receptionist was making such a big deal about. Hasn't she got better things to think about in her whole life?

We make eyes with Mum and Pops a few rows ahead and then settle down, but looking around I don't feel settled at all. All I see is lots of mums and dads and little dancers all scared and nervous and believing and hoping that they are best. I feel sick. I don't see a single person dressed like Poppy. All these girls are wearing leotards and have their hair scraped back. It feels like we are in the wrong room.

I whisper to Dad, 'Are we in the wrong room?'

He whispers back, 'No.'

I whisper back, 'I wish we were.'

He whispers back, 'Me too.'

252

The first dancer is like a swan, elegant and bendy and stretchy and so long like an everlasting ruler.

The second dancer is the same, and her feet are so quick like she is a jotty little needle on a sewing machine.

The third dancer is a bit crazy but still very impressive, and I know this because a few people even gasp.

It went on and on and on and on and on and on and on for at least three hundred and seventy-five years, so long I can't tell who is good and who isn't, and the whole time all I am knowing is Poppy is going to stand out like mad and that it doesn't seem that anybody here likes cowgirls or even Fred Astaire, and nobody else has a costume, let alone a water pistol, and I am panicking, my heart is screaming and I am so scared and want it to all be over. I am closing my eyes so tight they are all wrinkled up and I am wishing and wishing and wishing, and then I hear Poppy's music and it's time.

She does the dance absolutely perfectly, better than ever. The room is gigantic and the song sounds so excitingly splendid on the mahoosive speakers and the lights are all real like at the theatre, and they are shining all over Poppy, twinkling her sparkly suit and making star shapes all over the room. I am so proud and so into it, my whole body is pounding to her steps, and the feel of it is so tingly and wonderful and it feels so good to see my sister shine.

And then comes the grand finale. She gets the water pistol and she presses the trigger, and at the

same time the music goes right off and a long thick stream of water spits one of the judges right in the face. Some of it hits one of the other girls in the front row too. Everybody loses their breath in shock for a moment, and then Poppy laughs so cheekily and bows, and I wait: I wait for everybody to leap up and give her a standing clap like what happens on *The X-Factor*, and cheer and cheer, and the judges to get on their knees and say, 'We don't normally do this, in fact, Poppy Burdock – to be brutally honest,

255

it breaks every law in the audition handbook, but your audition today was not an audition, it was simply a *phenomenon* and it gives me great pleasure to offer you a place at our dance school . . . In fact, we are *begging* you.'

But all I hear is just a few awkward slow claps and coughs.

Then all of a sudden, the other audition girl who got a bit splashed with the water pistol jumps up and cries

to her mum like a massive show-off baby, and in a lispy hissy voice shouts, 'She's ruined my make-up, Mummy. Mummy, she's ruined it.'

And I'm thinking, *It's only water, you idiot, and besides you're about five, why are you even wearing make-up?* But everybody else isn't: they are tutting and shaking their heads and sniggering and whispering, and Dad goes, 'Oh dear,' in my ear.

But then he starts to really laugh. He laughs more and more, and I go, 'Dad, Dad, why are you laughing? Dad, poor Poppy, everybody hates her, Dad.'

And he doesn't stop, he just holds my hand so tight and says, 'What a bunch of snobs.'

Chapter Sixteen

We go to Pizza Express for dinner as a treat. I have an American and Dad has an American Hot. Mum has a posh one, Hector has a Margarita with extra tuna and Poppy has *whatever* she wants, which is a bite of Margarita, two slices of chocolate fudge cake and a gallon of apple juice.

It's weird. It's that feeling that even though the dance school have not actually said *yes* or *no*, we all know that Poppy did not get past the audition today, and actually it sort of doesn't matter. And even though she has been rehearsing for what feels like for an ever, and Mum made the costume and everything, it sort of is OK.

258

Poppy got her rejection
letter this morning. We know
because Mum tells Poppy, 'Just
read the first line and then we'll

forget about it,' and Poppy reads out: 'We regret
to inform . . .'

I suggest, 'What if it says, "We
regret to inform you that you left
your coat at the dance school
but you have a place here,
so just come and collect it
on your first day. Laters,
woop woop."'

Mum replies wearily, 'It doesn't work like that,
Darcy.'

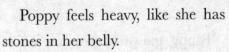

Poppy feels heavy, like she has stones in her belly.

'They were a bunch of snotty idiots,' Dad says. 'I'm glad she's not going there, Mollie.' (That's my mum's real person name.)

'I know, I know.' Mum gives her own head a rub.

'It's a load of rubbish,' Dad grunts, and starts looking in the fridge for delicious things.

'We couldn't have afforded it anyway,' Mum sighs. 'And it doesn't mean Poppy won't be a dancer one day.'

'Nothing will stop that,' I add, and Mum smiles to me and says, 'You're a good sister.'

I decide that Lamb-Beth can sleep in Poppy's room tonight because Poppy is a bit sad and is being more quiet than a chair.

I think it's so funny when the ones that *aren't*

like everybody else are the ones that *don't* get picked. I think the world is really upside down in that part. Don't people want to celebrate being special and unique? I will never get my head around that, but I know that Poppy didn't get a place in the school because she was *different* and that will for ever itch my brainbox.

I decide to write something about being special, and it sort of is for Poppy, but it's really for anybody that ever feels glum.

What Makes You You

In a world with so many
It's easy to feel a nobody.
Sometimes you can get blended in
With absolutely everybody.
But fear not,
For when you feel like this
Just go and find a quiet spot
And have a read of this . . .

So you have a spot on your chin,

Bobbly bumps on your skin

But you're easily the best at imagining.

So you have an upturned nose,

(Not even a little one either,

   like a real pig snout)

But without a doubt

You are the best to have fun with.

So your hair is pretty greasy,

Your fringe is wallpapered to your head,

But do you know what I call a greasy fringe?

   A gringe.

And they are in fashion . . . or at least, let's

   pretend.

So you have bitten thumbs,

Big gums,

A massive bum.

So has J-Lo and I don't see her complaining.

So you've got a horse mouth,

A uni-brow,

A chin that always goes into a frown,

A smile that's always upside down,
Cheeks so pink you look like a clown,
You also have a heart that is honest and true.

So you may have
So many flabby rolls it's like your
belly is a bakery.
Who cares, frankly?
Or maybe you're moley and freckly,
Got knobbly knees?
So tall it's like your
feet are overseas?
So skinny you can fill your
collarbone with a can of Coke?
Ears so big it's a practical joke,
Hairy back,
Hairy belly,
Hairy arms?
It adds to your
charm
That you're always
so sweaty

(And probably helps if you decide you want
   to go to a fancy-dress party as a wolf or
   a dog or a vole . . . you know, save on
   costume and that, you know . . .).

Maybe you're as blind as a
   mole?
Are your teeth as long as
   remote controls?
At least you got character.

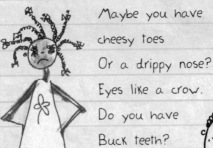

Maybe you have
cheesy toes
Or a drippy nose?
Eyes like a crow.
Do you have
Buck teeth?
Or
No teeth?

Or

Tiny baby milk teeth?

Do you have

Gap teeth?

Or

Brace face?

Or

Thousands of fillings all over the place?

Are you a bit silly?

Do you have . . .

Mud-stained shoelaces?

A fluffy tongue?

Veiny thighs?

A chubby tum?

Boss eyes?

Cross-eyes?

Eyebrows so high you
always look surprised?

Cankles . . . ?

Who knows what cankles are?

'Cankles' are when there is no direct thinning
between the calf and the ankle – you know,
where the whole leg sort of rolls into one?

CANKLES comes from the
fusion of the 'CA' from
calves and the 'ANKLE'
from *ankle*.)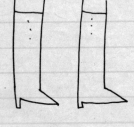

The only cure for cankles is
to wear boots,

So if you've got cankles, then guess what?

Good for you!

So if you are like me

(Had to have your
mum make clothes
for you out of old
curtains

And then would embarrass you
by picking you up from school
with her entire shirt open),

Or maybe you have inherited
A jaw like a set of shears?
Are you forever trying to dance
Like Britney Spears?
Or are you blessed with
A widow's peak?
A sunburnt face
Like a peeling disgrace,
Like a fried egg on a smashed plate?

Got
Bitten nails?
Muffin tops?

Are you a complete geek that
Loves hip-hop?
You got holes in your
    socks?
(No, not because of any
    other reason
Than your toenails are so sharp and long

They have turned into blades and have scalped
   their way through the sock material.)
Who cares — you're not hurting anyone.
Yes, you have blisters.
Yes, you might have holes in your pants or
   knickers.
Yes, you often get up in the middle of the night
   to have a nibble on a Snickers,
Greedy.
Yes, you have Hannah Montana stickers . . .
Who am I to judge?
Budge a you-

Shaped hole into
The universe
   and
Behold your
   birthmark!
Love your scar!
It's a wonderful
   work of art.

Besides, if you cock your head
    it sort of looks like a heart –
Really.
You're passionate about art.
You're the best at the bumper
    cars
And you're smart.
You know loads about the sea
Even though you find it scary.
And when you're scared
You suck your thumb
Like a BIG FAT BABY,
But I happen to think it quirky.
You're a marshmallow
    chocolate firework tart.
You're a lemonade supernova.
You always make me sick because
I laugh too hard,
And pick me up when I fall over.
You're loyal; you're never late.
I would let you eat anything off my plate.

You help me with my maths.

You're selfless, you're generous.

You speak like you're a Royal Highness,

But you must

Never change the pieces of the puzzle that make
    you who you are,

No matter if you will or won't or don't or do,

As wonky, spiky, pokey, gangly, podgy as you
    are,

Those are the things that make you special, that
    make you YOU.

I decide this time, for once, that I am going to read this one out loud. I decide to read it to Poppy in her room with Lamb-Beth. I read and I read and I am so nervous and am realizing that this is the first time I have ever read anything that I have written all by myself from my mind to anybody ever. But I do it and I am scared and I am shaking and am oddly so nervous and it is so nice to be here in this moment doing all this, and when I finally finish I fall into Poppy's arms and hold her tight to let her know that she is still the best dancer I have ever seen.

And then we laugh our heads off at that brat with the lispy voice that got sprayed by the water gun, and then even harder remembering what Dad said, that after all, 'Dancing is for snobs.'

Chapter Seventeen

It's easy to get carried away with the sticky webs of life. Things move on and grow and change, but you must never be sad about the way something has happened.

The spider is my room has finally gone and it has left the fly in its web. I am not sure if maybe it wasn't its favourite flavour or maybe it was a generous gift for me? But I don't eat flies unfortunately.

My dad has decided for no reason that he would quite like to be a basketball player, except he is a bit short, and Mum is worrying about how to break the news to him.

Hector and Lamb-Beth have got excellent at

being devious together, and sometimes she has paint on her feet from where she has been making paw prints on paper with Hector outside. He feeds her fruit pastilles and thinks I don't know.

The Pinchers are the same. Donald recently came over and made cookies with us and actually wasn't *too* bad – if anything he was kind of *funny*. I am not too hopeful, but he actually could turn out to be maybe OK-ish.

Henrietta has got herself a dog, which makes me happy. His name is Kevin. Which is a stupid name for a dog.

Mrs Cyril has moved out. I don't know what happened, but all I know is she whizzed off on the back of a motorbike with a man with the longest beard I have ever seen. She went off into the night with her granny skirt wrapped high over her knees and didn't even have any shoes on, and Mum said she was sticking her fingers up in that way you're not meant to do at Cyril, who was chasing after her shouting, 'Wait!' *Good*, I think. *Good*.

Poppy's scar from sharpening her finger has healed. It's funny how skin is so magical and heals all by itself and just grows back like grass. It's funny how anger heals in the same way.

Will and I are riding our BMXs to the shops to buy some more marshmallows, as we toasted the first set on Mum's scented candle and they tasted like scented candle, and then Mum told us off and said we could have set the house on fire and really scared us, so we are buying some more and are planning on eating them rawly.

For the first time I see Jamie Haddock out of school. He doesn't live near me so I don't know why he is here.

'Ignore him,' I say through gritted teeth to Will. And we keep riding, heads down.

'Darcy!' Jamie calls. His face is in a deep purple rash, either from running or crying or jumping or holding his breath or something.

'Yeah?' I say, all defensive and short.

'Look. I wanted to give you this.'

He holds out my writing book. I want to punch him in the face Round Two, but I don't because he looks like he might burst into tears. I grip my handlebars.

'Darcy, I took your book and I'm sorry.'

'Yeah, I know, you posted it on the internet. Why did you do that?'

'I wanted to . . . I dunno. Hurt you, I guess?'

'Yeah, well . . .' I couldn't think of anything else good to say. Will puffs his body out like a big protective bear, but I could tell he didn't need to, Jamie was too upset.

'I read your book,' Jamie finally manages to blurt out.

'You did?' I am shocked. I feel so embarrassed, like I am naked in front of the world for a second.

'Yes, I know I shouldn't have. Sorry.'

'No, you should not have, Jamie, and you certainly should not have stolen it. That book is private.'

'Darcy,' he says, 'your book is amazing.'

'Whatever, Jamie, look, thanks for the book, I am glad you have given it back, but reall—'

'Please let me finish. I'm sorry it took me so long to give it back to you. I am a slow reader.'

'Jamie, OK – we've got marshmallows to buy and—'

'Let him finish, Darcy,' Will says, and nods to Jamie, and this makes him look like he might cry more.

'I admit, I took your book to make fun of you and take the mick, but the more I started reading . . . the more I—'

I can tell this is maybe the hardest thing Jamie Haddock has ever had to do in All Time. He is sweaty and trembling.

He gets his croaky voice back and starts again. 'I felt like I was flying away to a new land when I read your stories,' he says, and then he pushes the book into my hands and runs away as quick as he can down the road.

I call his name but he does not look back.

Later, I chew raw marshmallows and think. Marshmallows are always more dustier than how I want them to be. If I wanted to eat a handful of flour I'd go and do it. But somehow I can't stop tasting the feeling of sparkly sunshine in my mind, and it's not from sugar, it's because somebody said that reading my stories felt like 'flying away to a new land'.

And that, to me, really is all that counts.

Acknowledgments

Thank you to my agents, Cathryn Summerhayes and Becky Thomas, for getting their heads around my head, for being honest and for letting me always get us into trouble. Becky, you have been so incredibly brilliant over the last year, thank you.

To all at WME, and extra big thank yous to Isabella, Katy, Elinor and Laura.

I would like to thank my incredible 'Team Darcy' over at the Random Towers. My editor, Lauren 'The Buckles' Buckland, thanks for taking a huge leaping chance, for getting me, for the cakes, the dinners, and *that* donut. I want to work with you for ever. Andrea Macdonald, for the splashes of glittery gorgeousness that she seems to speckle over everything she touches. Lauren Bennett, for simply being, as Darcy would say, 'siiiiiiiiiiiiiiiicccccccccckkkkk.' Thanks to Dominica Clements for all the help with design, her giggle and soft voice has almost convinced me that I can sort-of hold a pen, thanks for making things a bit more real. Also Clair Lansley for design help. Thank you to Annie Eaton, you make me happy every time I see you. Philippa Dickinson, thank you for believing in me and for your leopard-print shirt - it really certified for me that Random House was the right publisher to work with. Harriet Venn, thank you for your time on the book and for our first chat over pink lemonade. Alex Taylor and Charlotte Portman, for organizing everything, for making me tea, for always making me welcome and looked after. Thank you to Sue Cook, Sophie Nelson and Kirsten Armstrong for the Darcy copy edit and proof reads.

Thank you to Pat Lomax and Claire Bord. I will always be grateful.

Thank you to The Southbank Centre and Booktrust for saying 'yes' right from the start.

To Kim Smith, Shanna Baynard and Kate Fitzpatrick for your extra 'no-reason-nothing-in-it-for-me' help, you are so kind.

To Penny, Gemma and Adele, for idea swirling with me. You know Darcy better than anyone.

Thank you to my beloved proof reader; Mollie Grosberg. You are the Queen of Song.

Thank you to my mum, Jaine, and my sister, Daisy, who have just been out of control on supporting me. I love you so much. Without you I just could never have ended up at all.

Thank you to my brother Hector for letting me dress him up as a girl, my dad for introducing me to writing and Maria for encouraging his, to Ramsay for his time and advice, Steve for looking after my mum, the support from my husband's family, my beautiful friends old and new, from Brixton to New York - you know who you are and I love you. Siobhan, growing up with you was an absolute pleasure - thanks for being my 'Darcy.'

And Daniel. I mean, *wow*.